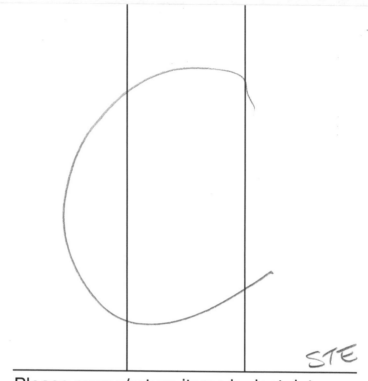

STE

Please renew/return items by last date shown. Please call the number below:

Renewals and enquiries: 0300 123 4049

Textphone for hearing or
speech impaired users: 0300 123 4041

www.hertsdirect.org/librarycatalogue
L32

George Washington Werewolf

a novel by

Kevin Postupack

Deep Kiss Press

George Washington Werewolf

ISBN: 978-1-938773-00-6

Cover design: AMERIKAN HIPSTER
Cover painting: Gilbert Stuart (1755-1828)
Back cover photos: Kerry Jacouac

www. DeepKissPress.com

Printed in the United States of America,
Canada, & the United Kingdom
10 9 8 7 6 5 4 3 2 1

Thanks to

Ashley DeAngelo (who made this a reality)

Seth Grahame-Smith (who made it a necessity)

Editor's note

George Washington Werewolf
is historically accurate.

(Except for the werewolves.)

Laborum dulce lenimen.

Latrante uno, latrat statim et alter canis.

"All his features were indicative of the strongest and most ungovernable passions, and had he been born in the forests he would have been the fiercest man among the savage tribes."

—Gilbert Stuart, Washington's portrait painter

December 1777
The Black Forest
(present day Germany)

The sound of horses' hooves against the frozen snow echoed in the crisp air, a frantic pounding as the carriage rider gave the poor lathering beasts the whip. The air was so cold it froze Bonndorf's nostrils to the point where he almost couldn't breathe. His chest hurt when he inhaled, like ice water poured into his lungs. His hands were sore from clutching the reins, his mother's wooden Rosary beads dangling from his fingers.

"Take the reins," he said, holding them out to Willy his young nephew. And as soon as Willy took hold, Bonndorf wiped his nose with his glove. Then he brought out the silver flask from within his heavy bearskin coat and put it to his lips. There it was, the warmth flowing down to his gut, radiating outwards through his body like rays of the sun. He turned to Willy and saw the clouds of breath coming from his mouth. The horses were racing, almost out of control. It was all Willy could do to hold onto the reins.

"Here, let me have them," he said. And within seconds they were going faster still. The moon was full and high in the sky, and everything was coated in layers of white, gray, and blue depending on the shadows from the forest. Sometimes the road was barely visible. At other times when the moon broke through the trees it lit up like daylight until every rut and pothole could be seen, like black pits in the snow and ice. But the full moon was exactly what Bonndorf was worried about.

The *Schwarzwald,* the Black Forest, was older than time itself, and for centuries the stories were told of the devils and demons, the creatures unearthly and undead who lived in these woods. Bonndorf had heard the tales, spun against firelight when he was a child, these nightmares in the form of bedtime stories that his parents told to him, to his brothers and sisters, these same stories that had been passed down through generations. So as he grew up he kept his distance from the woods because there were those who had gone into its shadows and were never seen again. But now as a grownup himself he had no choice. He ran a carriage service and the quickest route to most destinations was through the *Schwarzwald.* But every time he went beneath those trees, so old and sad and evil, he held the Rosary in his right hand (because the left hand was *sinistra,* as the Italians say), praying over each bead and then beginning again until the last tree was behind him.

And on the nights of the full moon he remembered the stories of what the French call the *loup-garou,* the man who turns into a wolf. The lycanthrope. The werewolf. No one he knew had ever seen such a creature, although the tales persisted through all the years he had lived by the forest. And when the moon was full the people here always stayed indoors. And then there were the slaughtered cattle, the horses and dogs, even he had seen those, and occasionally a man. Their bodies half-eaten, torn up, ripped to shreds, left in pools of blood the days following the full moon.

Again Bonndorf took out the whip. Holding it high overhead he brought it down on the horses' flesh, the sharp slap heard above the thumping hooves. He had a bad feeling tonight, something he couldn't explain, like when you find yourself in the middle of a dream that you can't escape from. A nightmare where you try to move but you're paralyzed, where you try to scream but only air comes out in soundless whispers. And then you feel it, the febrile skin, the desperately pounding heartbeat, the sweat against the sheets as you lie there motionless, at the mercy of whatever it is that's coming.

"We're almost there," he said to his nephew.

Bonndorf normally never took the coach out on a full moon, but this fare paid him three times the usual fee on the condition that they leave tonight and at once. Something about a matter of honor, an impending duel at dawn. And he could tell by a glance that this man had made the right decision, as most likely he wouldn't give a good account of himself if he kept his early morning appointment. And besides, Bonndorf needed the money. And with three times the pay he thought this job might finally put him ahead of the game. But now as the moon loomed overhead he began to regard the coins in his pocket less and less.

"We're almost there," he said again, although this time it was to assuage his own fears. A glance at Willy, at his nephew's face, his skin the ghostly pallor of mortified flesh. The naked limbs of the hardwood trees were skeletal hands reaching towards them. The sound of the wind, the moan of the frozen trees, the ice straining beneath the hoof beats were like something about to snap in two. He knew the horses couldn't keep up this pace for much longer, especially in this cold, but he kept hoping he'd reach the clearing that was still two miles away. Although right now he wished for it after every bend. He wondered to himself what time it was. Two in the morning perhaps? The time when even if one is safe in bed strange things are liable to happen. When you listen for a footfall and try to remember if you bolted the door shut before blowing out the candle. When your mind wanders to those places that are best left undisturbed, unvisited, as if just by you realizing this makes the worst things possible.

Bonndorf shook his head to dash these thoughts. Another mile, he said to himself, we can make it another mile. But suddenly the horses raised their heads in a peculiar way. They turned to the side as Bonndorf saw a shadow appear in the corner of his eye. And then there was a great collision! He felt it in the reins as the horses fell over themselves at full gallop. An agony of broken limbs and death cries as the coach careened forward until it struck the fallen beasts. Bonndorf felt himself hurtling through the air as he heard the screaming animals, the splintering wood crying out, and seconds later he was on the frozen ground against a tree. He saw the blood in the snow, blood from his forehead, and then the horrible mess of the dead mangled horses and the coach lying upside down in pieces, torn horseflesh hanging from its broken boards, the lifeless body of the man who had hired him amidst the debris.

"Willy!" he cried out. "Willy!" His nephew's name disappeared in clouds of breath. "Willy!" And then he saw his body crushed against a large boulder, the boy's limbs twisted into a position that only the dead can tolerate. And as he felt the tears forming in his eyes he saw the shadowy shape again, moving slowly by one of the horses. He watched it move methodically like some powerful beast as it tore into the horse's dead flesh. And at that moment a cloud passed from before the moon and light illuminated the scene. And as if feeling the moonlight the dark shape turned to face him. Bonndorf sat there in the bloody snow as these eyes that seemed to glow red pierced into his own, and deeper still, into his soul as the gray light revealed its shape. Like nothing he had ever seen, resembling a wolf but huge, muscular, with a large furry hump on its back and claws on its feet big as razors. And for a moment it stood there gazing at him through the moonlight, with a piece of what had been his lead horse in its mouth. And for a moment Bonndorf sat there petrified. He couldn't even breathe, and he might have been mistaken for a tree or an inanimate object had not the cloud of breath escaped his lips. The animal still fixing his gaze dropped the horseflesh onto the ground as its lips parted, as its teeth came together in a growl of such menace that Bonndorf felt his own hot urine stream through his trousers. This was no wolf. So the stories were true, he said to himself. He tried to close his eyes as the beast moved forward, but he couldn't. He was mesmerized, as if he were the prey now that gives itself up to the predator. He felt for the Rosary, but it was gone. And then he saw it a few feet away; the rosewood beads and the silver cross reflecting the moonlight, but then stomped into the snow as the creature took a step closer. Bonndorf stared at the clouds of breath coming from the beast's unholy mouth as it opened its jaws wide, and he heard the snow crunch beneath its feet as it leapt into the air.

January 1778
Port of Philadelphia
The New World

The *Auguste Villard* weighed anchor at Cherbourg the day of the full moon's wane. With twenty-seven days between full moons the voyage to America was made without incident in twenty-three, with barely a storm to speak of as it crossed the North Atlantic. And it was a beautiful sight as it dropped anchor at Philadelphia. Triple masted with lean lines and indigo with canary yellow trim, it was only four years out of the shipyard at Marseilles and the ocean still had not gotten the better of it. But the rumor was that one of its passengers was here at the behest of General George Washington, someone he hoped would turn the tide of war in favor of the Colonials (or those damned "Rebels", depending on where your allegiances lie). But since France was still officially neutral it landed without incident and was unmolested by the Redcoats, who had occupied Philadelphia since September of the previous year. And as the passengers disembarked and the cargo was unloaded a curious figure emerged, shouting orders at the deckhands, admonishing them to be careful as they carried what looked to be a large disassembled iron cage, followed by a slew of crates and divers baggage. But this was hardly unusual, considering the figure was decked out stem to stern in the tricorne hat, powdered wig, waistcoat, breeches, silk stockings, and buckled shoes of a nobleman. What *was* unusual was that the man who presented this figure was a dwarf of no more than three and a half feet in stature. And that he barked out orders and that they were obeyed meant that there was someone else, someone powerful behind him who the deckhands would answer to if they didn't hop to it.

And as the men made sure they didn't drop anything, one of the crew members, an able seaman named Vincent Bertin from Saint Gaultier, ran down the gangplank into the arms of his American wife of two years, Margaret Dorothea Bertin, nee Margaret Mayhew. "Of the Philadelphia Mayhews," she had joked when they first met. Her father was a saloonkeeper, her mother a laundress, and she was a seamstress. But now with two children she stayed at home to care for them as her husband was off at sea.

"Oh I've missed you so!" she said between kisses. "How was the voyage?"

"Uneventful," he said.

Vincent had learned English as a boy when his father apprenticed him to a shipbuilder friend in Liverpool, England. But after awhile the son realized that he was more the sailor than the builder and he signed on with *L'horizon,* a schooner out of Calais. And now he was with the *Auguste Villard.*

"Uneventful… That's good!" Margaret said.

"Well, except for…" he glanced over his shoulder at the dwarf.

"What? Who's that?"

"*Le nain?* I'll tell you later," Vincent said. "But first we'll go out and celebrate my return!"

"*Oui monsieur,*" his wife smiled.

And as they walked away Vincent turned once and stared at the dwarf, then looked up the gangplank to the ship as he expected someone else, someone he had heard about for twenty-three days at sea but had never seen.

10 pm
The Ram's Head Tavern
Philadelphia

The Ram's Head Tavern's wooden sign was relatively new. It was formerly the King George III, but Isaac Samuel Mayhew was a staunch supporter of the cause, meaning the Colonials, meaning what would become known as the American Revolution, and he took down the old sign on July 4th, 1776 and immediately put up a new one—The Ball & Musket. But last September after General Howe and his army of Redcoats 15,000 strong occupied Philadelphia, he chose the innocuous sounding Ram's Head Tavern, so he could cater to Rebel and Tory alike and not alienate the people who were suddenly in charge. But privately he would say he kept God and Country but got rid of the King (referring to the Loyalist motto of God, King, and Country). But if hard-pressed, he would confess further that he had replaced England with the Thirteen Colonies, this new country called America.

When his son-in-law Vincent Bertin walked into the tavern that night with his bride of two years, Isaac Mayhew greeted him as if he were the returning hero.

"A round of drinks on the house!" he proclaimed in his resonant baritone.

And for the next several hours Vincent and his wife Margaret sat at a wooden table soaked with beer, surrounded by friends and family toasting his return, toasting George Washington and the Continental Army.

"May the army stay together long enough for victory!" said one Langley McSwain.

"May the British go back to where they came from!" said Robinson Gwinnett.

"May the army stay together long enough so it outlasts the British!" said Isaac Samuel Mayhew, who was convinced that this was the only way the Rebels could ever win.

"Damn all Redcoats!" said another, and the tankards were raised again.

And from the other side of the tavern came sweet Loyalist voices together in song from a handful of Tories and Redcoats and a Captain of the 25th Dragoons...

"God save our gracious King..."

And in response from Vincent's table came boos and jeers, but then Isaac Mayhew stood tall, and holding a tankard in both hands he toasted in both directions (since people bought more beer when they were singing then when they were fighting). And his good-natured (albeit self-interested) gesture had a calming effect, and the two parties even raised their tankards to each other like one enemy ceremoniously regarding another.

"So you were going to tell me about that strange little man," Vincent Bertin's wife said.

"You mean Otto, the dwarf?"

"Yes, Otto the dwarf," she smiled.

"He came on board with some General or something..."

"A General?"

"From Poland I think. But we never saw him. We only ever saw the dwarf."

"That is odd."

"But what's even odder... is that a word?"

"Stranger."

"Ah!" he smiled. "What's even *stranger* is that Otto had us assemble this iron cage in the hold."

"An iron cage? What was in it?"

"That's just it... nothing!"

"Nothing?"

"*Rien!*"

"So what was it for?"

"Who knows! At least none of *us* knew. I'm sure that Otto knew, but the word was that if you crossed him you'd be sorry. That the General would..."

"What?"

"Well, that you'd disappear if you got in his way. And when you're in the middle of the North Atlantic that's easy to do."

"Disappear?"

Vincent Bertin nodded.

"So nobody ever saw him?"

"My you *are* curious!"

"I mend people's clothing, dear, and take care of the children while *you* sail off into the world!"

"Fair enough," he nodded.

"So this mysterious Polish General..."

Vincent tossed his hands to the side.

"And the cage was empty?"

"As far as I know," he smiled at his wife's enthusiasm. "And when we came into port, that... *homoncule* made us disassemble it and I kept looking for that Polish General but... then I saw *you* and..."

"And *I* was all you could think of!" Margaret smiled.

"Yes! *Exactement!*" he gave her a kiss. "I'm glad to be home."

"I'm glad as well," said Isaac Mayhew as he walked over and smiled at his son-in-law. "I'm glad you returned safely. Tell me Vincent, do you think your countrymen will join our cause?"

"Well, I wrote Lafayette asking him," Vincent smiled, "but I have yet to receive his reply."

Isaac Mayhew laughed and then raised his tankard again.

"To my son-in-law," he said, "able seaman Vincent Bertin!"

"To Vincent Bertin!" said the others.

"To France! To Lafayette!" And then, "Vive la France!"

And then from the other side, "To General Howe!" and "To His Majesty, King George the Third!"

By now everyone was too drunk to fight for King or Country (not to mention God), their arguments barely intelligible as the ale flowed until well after midnight. Vincent drained the last of his beer and then looked at his wife through the pewter tankard's glass bottom.

"*Tu est si belle,*" he said.

"What is that?"

"You are so beautiful," he smiled.

"Through your '*beer glasses*'," she smiled.

"No, *always!*"

"Hmm..."

"So we should probably go back home."

"Why, are you sleepy?"

"No," and Vincent leaned over. "*Je veux faire l'amour avec toi...*"

"Hmm?"

"Make love to me," he whispered.

"Monsieur! I'm shocked!" But she gave him a wanton smile.

Moments later they left the Ram's Head Tavern, hand in hand. And as they walked along the darkened street Margaret slipped on a patch of ice and Vincent caught her in his arms.

"Oops!"

"Thank you, my gallant gentleman."

"You are most welcome. Hic! *Je suis saoul...*"

"What?"

"I'm drunk," Vincent said.

"But not *too* drunk I hope..."

"Watch your step," he cautioned his wife.

And as they walked along the sidewalk they saw the moon overhead, hanging large and full in the sky directly above the steeple of the Dutch Reformed Church.

"Look at the moon!" Margaret said. "It's so big! Like we could go up to the steeple top and touch it. Do you want to?"

"What?"

"Come on! Let's go touch the moon!"

"I thought *I* was the one who was drunk," Vincent laughed.

And he watched his wife rush off towards the church, her eyes fixed on the moon. And as he hurried after her there was an otherworldly sound that echoed through the streets; something disconcerting and unusual for Philadelphia, like the howl of a wolf. But there was something pained and agonized about it as well, like the scream of the damned. And this was what Vincent Bertin thought of as his wife walked past an alleyway between buildings two blocks from their home.

"Margaret!" he called out. "Margaret!"

And as she turned around, a shape came from the shadows. It latched onto Margaret Bertin and like that his wife disappeared into the alleyway.

"Margaret!" he cried out.

He ran through the icy street to the alley. And as he turned he saw something barely visible beneath a shard of moonlight, making its way down the darkened corridor of brick.

"Margaret, is that you?" he asked. "Margaret? *Mon Dieu!* What happened? Where *are* you?" And as he stepped forward, his feet unsteady on the frozen water dripping from the roofs, he saw clouds of breath rising from a dark shape ahead, he heard what sounded like teeth crunching bone.

"Margaret?" he said again.

The next day the Philadelphia papers all ran the same story: Maniac on the loose. Two people found dead, their bodies unrecognizable, mutilated beyond description. Their souls commended to God's hands.

21 February 1778
Valley Forge
Pennsylvania

Snow had fallen during the night—not very much, just an inch or two, but enough to give everything a sense of newness like a fresh coat of paint. But the reality beneath the snow was of something quite different. Hardship. Deprivation. Disease. Starvation. These were the words George Washington used in his communiqués to the Continental Congress, in exile at York after fleeing Philadelphia last fall. He entreated them, he exhorted them, he begged and pleaded for supplies, for food, for clothing. He even used his own money because as it was now, Valley Forge for the Rebels had become the low point of the war.

The Continental Army went into winter quarters in early December when Valley Forge itself was just frozen ground, a densely wooded ridge sloping upwards from the Schuylkill River to the foot of a modest hill named Mount Joy. And the irony of that name was not lost on the 10,000 or so troops as winter set in and the icy rains came. After fortifying the ridge with entrenchments, artillery was placed on the high ground and the camp itself was secured. And then the enlisted men went about the business of chopping down trees to build the over one thousand huts they would live in by the New Year. And now by late February as the winter dragged on, General George Washington was giving in to despair. Almost 2000 soldiers had died since

December of disease and exposure as the Army had marched into Valley Forge in rags two months earlier, many soldiers barefoot, their uniforms in tatters, and still no supplies had arrived. And it was not unusual to hear General Washington pacing in his tent, railing against God and the heavens but mostly against the Continental Congress after receiving another letter informing him of yet another delay, demanding even more sacrifice. And then there was the constant hunger. Many men had starved and their horses had been slaughtered for food, which was a welcome change from the daily diet of a tasteless flour and water concoction called "fire cake". And because of all this, officers resigned and enlisted men deserted. The penalty for desertion was one hundred lashes but still the men ran off—to be with their wives and families, to be rid of the war—but on this day, after more bad news from York, General Washington himself ordered that a chronic deserter recently returned to camp be hung by the neck in full view of his troops, as an example and a warning.

The man was Private Josiah Cobb Whitlock of New Haven, Connecticut and this was the seventh time he had deserted and been brought back. And as the men assembled in the new-fallen snow before the makeshift gallows, General Washington and his senior officers sat on their mounts as Colonel Aaron Burr brought out the prisoner.

"We are gathered here today to mete out justice," said Colonel Burr. "We are fighting this war for our freedom and for the freedom of our country, and this man has repeatedly dishonored this noble cause. Do you have anything to say?" he asked the prisoner.

All eyes were on Private Whitlock. Stripped of his uniform in the rags of a prisoner he stood barefoot in the snow.

"God save King George," he said. And Aaron Burr stepped forward and slapped him across the face. He then looked to General Washington.

"You may proceed," Washington said, his expression impassive, fixed like a stone showing only his unshakeable resolve to see this through and to inspire his men to do likewise.

"Then may God have mercy on your worthless soul."

Colonel Burr motioned to Captain Tyler to lead the prisoner up the scaffold and put the rope around his neck, and then he nodded his head. Moments later Private Whitlock was dangling in the air as snow flurries descended and stuck to his body like quicklime. Nothing more was said. The men were dismissed. A half hour later the Private's body was taken down and buried in a shallow grave outside camp at the foot of Mt. Misery, the hill opposite Mt. Joy.

And later in his tent beneath the ragged blue banner with the thirteen stars, George Washington was filled with remorse that it had come to this, that he had to execute one of his own men.

22 February 1778
Valley Forge

The sun was out and the snow looked like powder dusting the ground. General Washington's wife Martha had just arrived by coach from Virginia to celebrate her husband's forty-sixth birthday. A party was held at the Potts House in the tiny village of Valley Forge and a band made up of soldier musicians played gay tunes. But no one could mistake the General's solemn countenance. And later, after the gathering dispersed, the commander confided in his wife his deepest fears.

"I cannot see us surviving this winter," he said, "if we're not re-supplied. We have barely seven thousand men fit for duty. The rest are sick or in the hospital or..."

"What?" his wife asked.

"Despondent," he said. "We... We can't outlast..." and he looked away.

"Come here," Martha said, and she held him close. "You're doing all that you can. More than *anyone* could have done."

"But those... those *men*," he said, the word almost spit from his lips, "those men in Congress. They're to be our ruination! They sit in their comfortable hotel rooms with their ample meals and full bellies. They... They're not *here!*" he said, as if that were the sum of the argument. "I've told them what it's like but still they have no idea."

His face was red, and Martha noticed the veins bulging along his temples, his hands clenched into powerful fists.

"I… I've run out of words," he said.

"My dear, dear man…" Martha said, this the only comfort her husband had received since the winter began.

"But thank God for the Prussian," Washington said, with an expression that almost betrayed a smile.

"The Prussian?"

"Von Steuben. He arrives tomorrow. A late birthday gift," the General smiled. "I'm hoping that… I'm hoping that… well…" He let out a breath.

"I'm hoping that too," Martha said.

23 February 1778
8 am

Even Washington had heard the stories. Von Steuben was an eccentric. A prima donna. After all, one of his demands was a private hut on the edge of camp far away from anyone else. And the hut had to be 15' by 15' square made of black spruce with no windows and its front door facing east. Also he was never to be contacted by anyone no matter what. If Washington needed to speak with him he was to be reached through his aide-de-camp who happened to be a dwarf. And there were other stories: that he had killed three men in duels; that he had tamed a wild bear and kept it as a pet; that he had an affair with Catherine the Great the Empress of Russia, and that he had killed the leader of the Cossack Revolt as a personal favor to her. But Washington didn't care. He was desperate. The army was falling apart and the word was that Von Steuben, known as The Baron, was the only one who could put it back together. (Although the "von" in his name and his title itself had been the subject of debate in Europe, regarding their authenticity.)

But what was beyond question was that he had been a veteran of numerous military campaigns, that he was a personal friend and advisor of Frederick the Great, and that his knowledge of military matters was unparalleled. And to top it off, Washington received a letter of recommendation from Benjamin Franklin himself praising the Baron as "the most renowned and honored Lieutenant General in the King of Prussia's service". So this was it, the last best hope as Washington put the future of the Revolution into the hands of this strange man. But George Washington felt a curious sense of anxiety, the "butterflies in the stomach", as well as a darker sense of apprehension, as he awaited Von Steuben's arrival.

23 February 1778
2 pm

Private Malcolm Turner—"Mal" to his friends—had spent three long years in the Continental Army. He was there at the defeats: Kip's Bay and Long Island. And the victories: Trenton and Princeton. Having grown up in Boston he saw the Revolution's beginnings. But now, three years later and with no end in sight, he was tired, hungry, and discouraged. And the "demonstration" the other day (the hanging of Private Whitlock) did little to amend his view.

"So what did you think of our little bit of entertainment yesterday?" he asked his friend, Private Solomon Bundy.

"What did he expect?"

"Who, Whitlock?"

"Yeah. I heard he deserted over twenty times."

"Twenty? I heard it was ten."

"What difference does it make? They have the right to hang you if it's only once!"

"Well, they may have the right, but that doesn't *make* it right."

"Tell that to the hangman."

"But still, to see him like that, twitching like some spastic cripple... the way his legs jerked. And then, did you see it? The stains in his breeches?"

"Hmm…"

"He peed and shit himself!"

"That's what happens, when…"

"But still, the lack of dignity. It was… disgraceful."

"That it was…"

"I tell ya, if they ever hang *me* I'm not gonna eat or drink a *thing* the day before!"

"*That'll* show 'em!"

"But still, I mean… I heard he had a wife and seven children."

"We're not here for fun," said Solomon Bundy. "We're here to win a war."

"By hanging our own soldiers…"

"Well… I see you got new boots."

"Yeah."

"Lucky dog."

Mal Turner offered a half-hearted smile.

"Speaking of, there was this dog the other day, did you see it?"

"No."

"It was black with these white spots…"

"No I said."

"Well, we ate it."

"You ate it?"

"Yeah, we shot it in the head and had it for supper. It wasn't bad. Better than fire cake. Did you hear about Burr?"

"Burr?"

"You know Captain Dickenson?"

"Dickenson? I haven't seen him in a while."

"That's because Burr chopped his arm off!"

"What?"

"He disobeyed a direct order, Dickenson that is, and Burr took out his sword and sliced it right off! His arm, I mean. And the poor bastard looked down at his own arm lying there in the snow!"

"Jesus!"

"Yeah."

"Were you there?"

"No, but Smythe was. You know Ben Smythe? He's from Maine. Isn't that near Boston?"

"Ha!"

"But can you picture it?" Bundy went on. "This chopped off arm lying in the bloody snow! That kills me! And it's even better since Dickenson was such an ass!"

"So where's he now?"

"Some hospital I guess."

"So what happened to Burr?"

"Ha! I guess he'll get another promotion!"

"Hmm."

"So I haven't seen Dil around lately..."

"Dil?"

"Your friend, Dilburton..."

"Hmm..." Mal let out a sigh. "He died of pneumonia last week."

"Sorry."

"These are his boots..."

"Well, that's a good inheritance," Solomon Bundy said. And after a pause, "So if you die can *I* have 'em? The boots I mean...

And they both looked at Bundy's feet, at his worn-out shoes that were nothing but strips of leather held together with pieces of twine.

Mal nodded his head.

"Thanks Mal... So what do you think o' this big wig who's coming to camp?"

"You mean *'The Baron'*..."

"Yes, *'The Baron'*..." Bundy smiled.

"I heard he's from Hungary or Prussia or somewhere, and that he can't speak a word of English."

"I heard he can't speak at all because he had his tongue cut out when he was captured by Cossacks, and that they fried his tongue in animal fat and fed it to their wolfhounds."

Mal smiled. "I heard that he travels with his half-brother who's a midget."

"Speak of the Devil…"

"Well I'll be damned!"

And the two soldiers watched as a well-dressed dwarf led a detachment of troops carrying all sorts of baggage.

"What the Hell is *that?*" Bundy asked.

"It looks like a cage."

"What, did he bring a pet lion?"

"I guess."

"That's a lot of stuff!"

"Generals…"

"Well, you keep at it Mal. Maybe by the time the war is over you'll be a Corporal."

"Thanks."

"Oh look, there's Burr trying to look all imposing and self-important."

And they watched as Colonel Aaron Burr observed the processional, a look of barely disguised envy on his face.

"Look! I guess that's him," said Bundy. "The Baron himself!"

Not as tall as General Washington, but still there was something utterly commanding in Von Steuben's bearing. He carried himself like a cross between an aristocrat and a killer, which was a dangerous combination. And as he walked through camp the men stood aside in a kind of reverence or awe, as if he were the King of Prussia himself.

"Those Redcoats have had it now!" exclaimed Solomon Bundy.

"We'll see…"

"Hey, you know what today is, right?"

"What, George Washington's birthday?"

"No, it's mail day!"

"That's right!" Mal broke into a smile.

"So maybe you'll get another letter from… what's her name? Alma? Abigail?"

"It's Lenore, but you were close."

"So I'm gonna go and see what I got, all right? I'll see ya later Mal…"

"See ya Sol."

"Keep warm!"

"You too."

And Private Malcolm Turner looked back at The Baron and then at the men carrying the huge iron cage. What could that be for, he wondered. What could that possibly be for?

23 February 1778
4 pm

The mail had arrived and Mal Turner had received a letter from Boston from one Lenore Weston, but for some reason he had a sinking feeling as he opened the wax seal. He sat on his makeshift bunk in the log hut he had helped build back in December, when he and Lenore had talked about getting married. But since then he had received only two letters, and not once did she mention their forthcoming marriage. He took a deep breath as he looked at her words, written in a steady determined hand.

27 January 1778

Dear Malcolm,

I am sorry to have not written much lately, but I wanted to make sure of something before I finally told you. I regret with all my heart that I have met someone else. He is a merchant in Boston who owns his own ship, but mainly he is here and is staying here and you have been away for so long. I don't know when this war will ever end and I don't want to postpone my life any longer, as I want to have children. Please forgive me, as I do care for you, and I hope that the war is soon over so you may one day be as happy as I am now.

Yours in friendship,

Lenore

"Bad news?" Berkeley, one of the enlisted men asked as he passed by.

Malcolm Turner tried to speak but he had lost his voice. He started to crinkle up the letter but he couldn't bring himself to do so. Instead, he placed it gently on the bed and then turned away, a single tear forming in the corner of his eye.

23 February 1778
9 pm
The Potts House
The Village of Valley Forge

Isaac Potts built this house out of stone thirty years before, when all was right with the world, when the Colonists were happily British, and this Revolution was not even a glimmer in the most radical mind. But tonight it was the scene of a gala party in honor of Baron Friedrich Von Steuben, who had traveled from Prussia through the Black Forest to France, and then across the Atlantic to Philadelphia to Valley Forge to save General Washington and his ragtag army from defeat.

"Baron..." George Washington said as he executed a deep stately bow.

"General..."

"My wife, Martha..."

"Mrs. Washington..."

And as Martha Washington looked at the face of this man who was to be their savior, she couldn't help but notice the resemblance to her husband George. Though shorter he bore a not dissimilar countenance, and could be mistaken in a certain light as perhaps a brother or a cousin. And perhaps this was why the General and the Baron instantly took a liking to each other. Both were men of wealth and privilege who chose the soldier's life. Both had seen their share of battles and of dying men. And now General Washington hoped that this would be the first step towards ending this war and securing American independence. He saw in the Baron's face a kind of indomitable strength and will, but yet something more as he looked deeper, as his eye aided by the many glasses of wine glimpsed something untamed and dangerous. But this was precisely what they needed. The men had grown tired, complacent, weary of war, and filled with a longing for home. He hoped that this man would somehow make them want to fight again, and make them want to win.

"My husband has told me all about you, Baron," said Martha Washington. "So many interesting tales!"

"And perhaps one or two are even true," the Baron smiled.

At this one of Isaac Potts's dogs, a large Alsatian named Romulus, trotted into the room, but it stopped abruptly as it peeled its lips and growled at Baron Von Steuben. The dog looked him right in the eye, a look of challenge and fear even, and it seemed as if it were about to attack when a well-dressed dwarf kicked the beast in the ribs and told it in no uncertain terms to be gone.

"Forgive me," said Washington, "the owner of the house, his dog..."

"Quite all right."

But Martha Washington looked at the Baron for a moment longer, sensing something peculiar, something odd, and suddenly she felt an unsettled feeling in her stomach.

"What is it dear?" Washington asked. "You look peaked."

"Do I? It must be the rich food."

"No, it's because Mrs. Potts is nowhere near the cook that Mrs. Washington is!" the General said as an aside.

"Hmm, my kind sir," Martha bowed, and then she turned to the Baron. "Well, I'm sure that you and my husband have many things to discuss," she said, as she begged her leave.

"A charming woman," said Von Steuben.

Martha Washington left their company and as she came into the drawing room she saw Romulus the dog, and she bent down to pet his head.

"What is it boy? What's wrong?"

The dog nuzzled up to her, licked her face, gave its tail a wag, but then stood at attention as it stared into the other room, its eyes fixed again on the Baron. A low measured growl rumbled through the dog's body and into her hand as she stroked its flank, and Martha Washington stared at Von Steuben with the same incredulous scrutiny.

"So I hope your quarters are to your satisfaction..." George Washington said.

"They are, General. And to ease your mind I will begin at first light to shape your men into an army."

"I hope they weren't too embarrassing a sight upon your arrival..."

"Not at all, General!"

But Washington saw in his expression that this was not quite true.

"But tonight let us celebrate your arrival, Baron!" Washington exclaimed.

"Yes, because from tomorrow on it will be all business. Have you met Otto?" the Baron asked. "My aide-de-camp..."

Von Steuben motioned downward at the dwarf. And there was the marvelous moment as the six foot three General Washington bent down to shake hands with the three foot six inch dwarf.

"A pleasure, sir," said Washington.

"The pleasure is mine," Otto replied.

"Otto is my right hand," said the Baron. "My confidante, my protector, my friend, my... how do you say? My confessor?"

And George Washington couldn't help but smile, that this very small person could be so many things including the protector of such a formidable figure as Baron Friedrich Von Steuben. At this, Colonel Burr walked over.

"Baron Von Steuben, may I introduce to you one of my most talented officers, Colonel Aaron Burr..."

"Colonel Burr..."

"Baron..."

"I'm sure you will be seeing more of me than you would like over the next several months," Von Steuben smiled.

"It will be my honor, sir."

"But for now I must discuss things with your General..."

"Of course, sir."

"Good night, Colonel."

"Good night, Baron."

"So what did you want to discuss?" Washington asked.

"Nothing," the Baron smiled. "He just seems like a very serious man."

"Colonel Burr? Yes he is."

"Tomorrow I will be serious," said Von Steuben. "Tonight I will be gay!" he emptied his glass. "This wine is excellent, *mon Général!*"

"Yes, your friend Mr. Franklin sent us ten cases from Paris."

"Ah, my good friend Ben! His taste in wine is exceeded only by his taste in young women..."

"Hmm..." Washington smiled.

And the night was spent drinking some of the finest wine in the New World. And by evening's end when General Washington retired to his bed, he was enamored of the Baron and was convinced that this mysterious man, Friedrich Von Steuben, held within him the seeds of Great Britain's defeat. Whereas Martha Washington, her eyes closed feigning sleep, still could not shake that feeling of disquiet and foreboding.

24 February 1778
6 am
Valley Forge

Out of the early morning mist rode a man who seemed larger than life, as if he were Mars, the God of War himself. Dressed in full martial regalia, polished boots, gold braided epaulettes, medals galore, pistols at his side, saber in hand, a purple plume rising from his hat, Baron Friedrich Von Steuben faced the assembled American soldiers for the first time. And what he saw came as a shock: haggard, unshaven, gaunt, tatterdemalion, with no semblance of military order, discipline, or decorum. Yet there was something about these hardy disheveled souls that deeply impressed him. They were not professional soldiers in it for the money as he was accustomed to in Europe, nor were they mercenaries like the Hessians, but rather simple volunteers. Farmers mostly, here for no other reason than the cause in which they believed. "In Europe," he told Washington later that day, "no professional army could have been kept together under such impossible circumstances. But here in America there apparently is a different kind of man."

The Baron believed in teaching by confrontation, as he dismounted and strode right up to one of the soldiers, an especially pathetic-looking Private named Merriman. Private Mal Turner who was only a few feet away, looked on and took a deep apprehensive breath.

"WHAT'S YOUR NAME, PRIVATE?" the Baron shouted.

"Private Ambrose Patrick Merriman, Inspector General, sir!"

And with his face inches away the Baron shouted at the top of his lungs, "COME TO ATTENTION, SOLDIER! HEAD UP! CHIN IN! CHEST OUT! STOMACH IN! SHOULDERS BACK!" punctuating each command with a slap of his swagger stick. And there was something in his demeanor, in his expression and his eyes that told the men that he was not to be tested, that they should snap to his every command, as by now the rumors had circulated that he had once executed an entire squad of his own soldiers who showed cowardice in the face of the enemy, and that he had pulled out an enemy soldier's eyeball with his own fingers during battle.

Von Steuben then directed his gaze on the men at large, and if they didn't feel the lump rise immediately to their throats then they were no good liars or laggardly goldbricks who didn't deserve independence in the first place.

The plan was simple. Drill the men like they had never been drilled before, until their feet ached and their legs were about to fall off and they cursed the day Von Steuben was born and they were all ready to collapse but didn't; until they marched in their sleep and deployed into line of battle in their dreams; until they could fire their weapon, reload, then fire again with the effort it takes to breathe; until they moved together as a single mind, with a single purpose, of defeating the enemy.

At first the men were resistant, since Von Steuben's method resembled torture not training. And when the Baron realized that the men didn't understand his curses in German he appointed a bilingual aide, one Corporal Johannes Hesse, to translate his most foul and abusive German epithets into the most foul and abusive English ones, and in spite of it all by the end of the first week the soldiers were taking pride in themselves and what they had accomplished. They would even come to watch the other companies drill, hoping to look that good themselves when it was their company's turn on the field. And General Washington himself could not hide his pleasure at the progress being made. It was two and a half months until May when they would re-engage the British Army. For the first time he thought there was a chance they might be ready.

1 March 1778
9 am
Valley Forge

The day had come for Martha Washington to return to Mount Vernon, to Virginia. Her carriage had arrived and her baggage had been stowed and now there was the matter of the tearful good-bye. She had no idea when she would see her husband again. As much as she held out hope in the new prospects for victory she held onto her suspicions. And it was with trepidation that she stood now before her husband.

"I will miss you, dear," she said.

"And I you," George Washington said with a soft smile. "At least the weather is fair."

"Yes, it is quite mild this morning."

"I will do my utmost to... to come home soon," he said.

"I know you will."

And as they gave each other a final hug, Martha leaned over and whispered something in her husband's ear...

"Be careful!" she said. "Watch out for the Baron... There's something not right."

1 March 1778
4 pm
Valley Forge

"You look terrible!" said Private Solomon Bundy.

"Thanks," said Malcolm Turner. "I have this cold."

"Well, you're lucky."

"How is that lucky?"

"Because *I* feel terrible and I'm not even sick. It's Von Steuben. All that bloody drilling. Drill, drill, drill! My legs are ready to fall off! But I *did* learn one thing though. Look…" And he took his musket with bayonet fixed and brought the long blade into the heart of a nearby bale of straw. "Take *that*, General Howe!"

Mal only had strength enough to nod his head.

"Sorry about… Lenore…"

"Thanks."

"But you're better off."

"How am I better off? She's in some nice warm house in Boston with some man who owns his own *ship!* I'm stuck here…"

"Well, you're a hero, right? When we win this war we'll have our pick of the pretty girls! So did you hear about Von Steuben?"

"What now?"

"I heard that he murdered two Redcoats while he was in Philadelphia… with his bare hands! And that they couldn't even be identified."

"Well I heard that Baumgartner… Do you know him?"

"Yeah, he's a Corporal, right?"

"Yeah, I heard that he went to see Von Steuben…"

"At his private hut?"

"Yes!"

"Oh God!"

"And that the midget shot him dead!"

"You mean Baumgartner?"

"Yeah, he shot him in the head with a flintlock. And then he had his body thrown in the river."

"Hmm. If I've learned anything in the two weeks that old Prussian's been in camp it's to stay as far away from him as possible…" said Solomon Bundy. "And that midget too!"

11 March 1778
10 pm
The outskirts of camp

Aaron Burr had always been an ambitious man. He graduated from Princeton at sixteen. Now at the age of twenty-two, a Colonel in the Continental Army as well as a confidante of General Washington, he had his sights set on becoming General. And then after the war, who knows? And the way to advancement was never to sit around and wait, it was to get up and *do* something. It also didn't hurt to know the right people. He happened to have been a brilliant scholar, but nevertheless his own father was President of Princeton College. And now the man to know was this Prussian Baron. So it was with this in mind that he set out through the woods, to the private hut of Friedrich Von Steuben.

Of course the men had been warned to not come within ten yards of this place, but Aaron Burr was used to doing what he pleased. In the woods he found the path used by the Baron himself, lit by the last of the waxing gibbous moon, as tomorrow night the moon would be full. The only sounds were his footsteps in the snow, as the camp sounds were muffled by the thick trees. But then he was startled by a loud "Hoot!" Instantly his pistol was drawn and pointed at a barn owl on a nearby branch, scrutinizing him with its strange black eyes in the middle of that round white face.

"Bang!" Burr said as he watched the bird fly away, and he returned the weapon to its holster.

Another hundred feet and he could see the hut up ahead through the trees. It was well constructed but as he got closer he noticed that there were no windows. When he reached the door instead of knocking he looked down at a strip of light coming from within. And although Colonel Burr was a confident man bordering on arrogant he couldn't deny the uneasy feeling he had now as he stood before that door. In fact at one point he thought about turning around, going back to camp, but then he took a breath and brought his knuckles against the hard wooden door... No answer.

"Inspector General?" he called out, his breath rising in clouds that quickly disappeared.

Another knock with no response and then he reached over, opened the door, and strode inside. There was a lantern shining out from a small table. As he looked around he saw that no one was there. But the thing that stood out was what occupied most of the space. The room was taken up almost entirely by a huge iron cage that sat in its center. There was just enough room on the perimeter for a few chairs, a table, an armoire (which Burr figured was from Europe because of its elaborate design), and a simple cot on a wooden frame. But his eyes kept coming back to the cage. He walked over and tried to move its bars but it was solid and strong. If someone were put inside they would not get out. But why was it here in the first place? Burr wondered.

At that moment he heard the unmistakable sound of a flintlock being cocked.

"What are you doing here?" came an odd, rather high-pitched voice.

"May I turn around?" Colonel Burr asked.

"But very slowly. My pistol is aimed at your head," came the voice, "and I am an excellent shot."

When Aaron Burr turned around he saw Otto the dwarf, Von Steuben's weird aide-de-camp. And he wasn't lying, as he held what looked like a beautiful French dueling pistol.

"Is that French?" Burr motioned to the flintlock held in the dwarf's small but pudgy hand.

"Italian… Bolognese."

"Ah, Bolognese!" Burr exclaimed. "Fernandez? Of Madrid?"

"Of course. 1727. You know your firearms, Colonel."

"May I see it?"

"Um, some other time," the dwarf said. "What are you doing here, Colonel Burr?"

"I was sent by General Washington… a matter of some urgency. Is the Inspector General anywhere to be found?" Burr's eyes kept returning to the cage.

"He is not, I'm afraid. I will however tell him that you called. And please, for your own safety, from now on you must contact me in camp and I will relay your message."

"Very well," said Burr.

"And I repeat, for your own safety."

Colonel Burr nodded. "May I go?" he asked.

"Of course," said the dwarf as he stepped out of the way, although his gun was still ready to fire.

Burr took several steps, then stopped and turned to the little man.

"Might I inquire as to the purpose of that… cage?" he asked.

"No, you may not. Good night, Colonel Burr. Be careful in the woods. I hear there are wild animals about… even wolves."

"Thank you, I will," Burr replied.

The moment he was outside the door slammed behind him. And there on the dead branch of a pin oak was the barn owl again, looking him right in the eye. Since he was a little boy he had heard that owls were bad luck. He brought out his pistol, this time to shoot it for real. But when he looked back at the tree the bird was gone.

11 March 1778
10 pm
The Groves Mansion
Philadelphia

Captain Ballistar Braxton of His Majesty's 25th Dragoons had grown bored with Philadelphia. He was determined to distinguish himself beyond the rank of Captain. Yet this was proving to be impossible since General Howe's army spent its time in winter quarters chasing one party after the next. Most of the men, from the Privates to the Generals, were anything but idle that winter. There was entertainment and distraction galore, of every conceivable kind.

Tonight the opulent mansion of the Loyalist Wavely Makepeace Groves was the place to be if you were a British officer. The men were in full dress uniforms, the women in their most alluring ball gowns, the string quartet playing the livelier numbers of Haydn, Vivaldi, and Corelli, the supply of wine, champagne, and whiskey inexhaustible. Yet Captain Braxton stood apart, observing it all with a kind of detached contempt until his friend Roland Montague walked over, obviously drunk, but blending in well with everyone else.

"Captain Braxton…"

"Captain Montague…"

"You're not drinking…"

"No, but I see you've done my share as well as your own."

"Yes, have you noticed what a fat pig Howe has become since last September?"

They both looked over at the General, a glass of wine in one hand, a turkey leg in the other.

"He must have gained a hundred pounds!"

"That's our Commander-in-chief you're talking about," smiled Braxton.

"I don't think he'll be able to fit on his horse come May!" laughed Montague. "Oh, look at that one!"

They turned to observe one of Philadelphia's young belles and her rather ample bosom exploding from her gown.

"Can you imagine her with Howe? My stomach is turning…"

"And there's Tarleton… what an ass!"

"But the ladies love him…"

"Apparently the ladies of Philadelphia have questionable taste."

"What a way to fight a war, eh Braxton old man? Parties every night. We'll all be too drunk and fat come the Spring. And meanwhile ol' Washington is just twenty miles away, starving and freezing his ass off. We should just ride up there and attack!" said Montague. "At least it'll give us something to do."

Braxton nodded his head in silence.

"Oooh! Look at *that* one!" Montague exclaimed. "You could *drown* in those!"

"So would you like to?" Braxton asked.

"What? Drown in those tits?"

"No, ride up to Valley Forge… attack Washington…"

"What? I was joking old man! I'm drunk, can't you tell?"

"Because I'm doing that exact thing tomorrow night," Braxton said in a voice that couldn't have been more businesslike.

"What? What are you talking about?"

"I've been planning this for weeks…" Braxton moved closer, speaking softly into Montague's ear. "I've put together a squad of men. We'll be dressed in rags like the Rebels and we'll appear at Valley Forge with four Hessian prisoners…"

"What? You want to attack Valley Forge?"

"Ssssh!" Braxton glanced around to see if anyone was eavesdropping, but the drunken revelers were oblivious. "We inform the pickets that we're a scouting party sent out under the explicit orders of Von Steuben…"

"Von Steuben?"

"He's their Inspector General now."

"I heard he's crazy! That he uses the severed head of a Russian Cossack as a paperweight…"

"This way their guards won't dare question our story, and we'll definitely *look* the part. And then we'll march right into camp with impunity, go up to George Washington's tent, and kidnap him!"

"Kidnap him? Have you lost your mind?"

"And then the Rebels will sue for peace and a week from now this war will be over! And we'll be heroes, you and I! The toast of London when we return!"

"Are you sure you're not drunk?" Montague asked.

"Sober as a bishop. So do you… do you want in?"

"Do I want *in?* Ha! You're *crazy!*" Montague laughed.

"We leave tomorrow morning at dawn."

"At *dawn?*" he shook his head, but then a smile came to his face. "Ahh, *I* get it. That's really funny, Braxton. You had me going there for a while."

At this a lovely young lady in a handsome blue gown with gold filigree walked slowly by and gave Captain Montague the eye.

"Well, I'm afraid duty calls, old man. Kidnap Washington! That's a riot!" And then he turned his attention to the passing brunette. "Good evening, mademoiselle," he said. "Captain Montague at your service…"

11 March 1778
11 pm
The Bunch of Grapes Tavern
Philadelphia

The Bunch of Grapes Tavern had always been just another place to drink, no better or worse than the hundred or so other bars in Philadelphia, but after the Occupation it had become the rowdiest and most explicitly bawdy place in town. Its owner, Sebastian Younger Cowles had always been loyal to the Crown and a bit of a brawler in his day. And it was perhaps for these reasons that the Grapes was packed each night with the most unsavory types: Redcoat enlisted men, lowlife Tories, and Loyalist sympathizers in the form of thieves, pickpockets, convicts, rogues, and politicians, as well as every manner of young lady of loose character and even looser garments. And tonight was no exception as Private Mandalay Fitzsimmons sat with his friends, as the beer flowed freely and the words flowed freer still.

"So you're saying by next week the war will be over?" said Sally Tompkins, who had found her calling during the British Occupation as a prostitute of much renown.

"Yes!" Fitzsimmons bragged. "And I will be toasted in this selfsame bar as a hero of England!"

"Is that so?"

"And me too!" said his friend Private John Wiley, who punctuated his comment by thrusting his entire face into the exposed bosom of Mary, the prostitute who sat immediately to his right.

"So the both of you are to be heroes then?" Sally smiled.

"That's right!" said Wiley as he came up for air. "We're going to introduce ourselves to General Washington himself! You know that Valley Forge is only twenty miles away…"

"I thought it was eighteen…" said Mary.

"You know soldiers," Sally smiled, "always saying things are longer than they really are."

The girls all laughed and the soldiers shook their heads and returned to their glasses of beer.

"So if you know so much why don't you come with us?" said Fitzsimmons.

"That's an idea," said Sally. "But I'd have to be in command."

"Of course! Just like my wife," he smiled.

"You're married?"

"Well, back in England…"

"That doesn't count!" said John Wiley.

"This is Philadelphia," said Private Fitzsimmons, "and what happens in Philadelphia…" He turned to Colleen, one of the barmaids. "More beer, darlin'!"

And the girl walked over and poured a tankard of ale all over her exposed bosom, and Mandalay Fitzsimmons cheerfully obliged by planting his face in her cleavage and lapping up the spilled brew.

"Mandalay, I have some beer for you as well!" said Sally Tompkins as she poured beer on her chest.

"What kind of name is Mandalay?" Mary asked.

"What?" Fitzsimmons turned around after finishing with Colleen.

At times you couldn't hear yourself think at the Bunch of Grapes, with all the racket of several hundred drunken roisterers shouting, laughing, singing, fighting, all done uproariously.

"I said what kind of name is Mandalay?"

"It's *my* name!" Fitzsimmons smiled. "Look, here comes another hero..." he motioned to the man who just walked in the door.

But before he could get to their table another man intercepted him.

"Denkins! I *thought* that was you!" said the other man, who followed this with a roundhouse haymaker that sent the prospective hero reeling against a table of revelers who took this as a personal affront. Within seconds, fists were flying and ten or so drunken soldiers were trying their best to beat each other up.

"Oh well..." said Fitzsimmons.

"So, you're married?" said Mary.

"That's okay, whenever I think of my wife I want to make love..."

"Ahh, that's so sweet and romantic," said Sally.

"To other women!" Fitzsimmons smiled.

And he grabbed Sally by the arm and spirited her to a nearby corner where he began to mount her against the wall, as his friends back at the table toasted his good fortune.

"So, you're really going to meet George Washington?" Mary said, wide-eyed.

"As God is my witness," said John Wiley. "There's this Captain of the Dragoons..."

"I *love* the Dragoons!" Mary gushed. "Their uniforms are so smart, so handsome! Is he coming tonight? This Captain of the Dragoons?"

"Colleen, more beer!" Private Wiley said.

A few minutes later Private Fitzsimmons reappeared at the table and demanded more beer.

"So how was he?" Mary asked in a whisper.

"Talk about *Minute Men*..." Sally Tompkins laughed.

"Do you think we should help him?" said Wiley. "Denkins, I mean..."

"Nah, he'll be fine," said Fitzsimmons.

"But maybe we should get back soon... I mean we have to be assembled at dawn."

"Maybe you're right. One more round!" Fitzsimmons bellowed.

"All right... So Mary, what do you say we go try out that corner?" Private

Wiley pointed to the spot where Sally and Fitzsimmons had just cavorted.

"If you wish, my Lord," she replied. And Wiley swept her out of her seat and started undoing his belt buckle.

By now the fight had subsided and Private Denkins stumbled over and sat down, a black eye and a bloody lip the price he paid for coming to the Bunch of Grapes this evening.

"Allow me to introduce you to Private Miles Danfield Denkins…" Private Fitzsimmons announced.

"So, another one of your heroes?" Sally Tompkins smiled.

13 March 1778
2 am
A full moon
The outskirts of camp
Valley Forge

Private Mal Turner had been feeling poorly ever since he got the letter from his fiancée breaking off their engagement and telling him that she was in love with someone else. At first he thought he was just heartsick. But today he knew it was something more as he stood there in the middle of the night in the middle of this downpour, burning up with fever. It had been raining since he started his guard duty at eleven, on the far side of the camp near Mt. Misery. He had tried to get somebody to cover his shift so he could go to bed. But who in their right mind would want to stand out in a pouring-down rain? Besides, what was the point? It was well known that the British were all happy, warm, and drunk as could be in Philadelphia, eighteen miles away.

For the past few hours, Mal hadn't seen or heard a soul. Everyone was asleep in their huts which, leaky roofs notwithstanding, were Paradise compared to this. The spring thaw was here as the ground had softened and turned to mud. The rain seemed to come down in sheets right into Private Turner's face, no matter where he positioned himself. And he even thought he had fallen asleep for a while standing up, as he was genuinely surprised when he looked at his pocket watch and saw that it was two in the morning. There was no telling how he would make it to six o'clock when his shift was over.

The rain showed no sign of letting up as he wiped his runny nose and then reached for his flask, taking a long sip of whiskey. And this was the real thing, from the Kentucky frontier, not that almost undrinkable poisonous mash that the soldiers made. His friend Solomon Bundy had given it to him as a get-well gesture after Lenore broke his heart. And as Mal finished his drink he looked at the flask. He'd better go easy if this were to last him the night. He glanced at the sky. The night was gray as a woolen blanket, the full moon completely obscured by clouds, as a cold drop of rain hit him like a steel pellet right in the eye.

"Damn all officers and gentlemen!" he said to himself, followed by a flurry of sneezes. "Only four more hours!" he laughed, with the black humor of all soldiers who are stationed in such miserable places as this.

And then from out of the rain and cold emerged a group of figures that looked like a band of Rebels. What was left of their ragged uniforms was soaked to the bone. Their boots or bare feet were caked with mud. And Mal looked over in bemused silence. At first he thought he was dreaming, thinking that he'd fallen back asleep. They were even sorrier looking than he was. And then one of them, in the remnants of a Captain's uniform, spoke through the rain.

"Captain Braxton with a detachment of Continental Soldiers under the direct orders of the Inspector General… We have four Hessian soldiers as our prisoners."

In response Private Mal Turner sneezed.

"Private, is it not customary for a subordinate to salute a superior officer?"

"Yes sir, of course sir!" Mal said as he offered a salute. "My apologies, Captain sir. I thought you were a dream."

"A dream? No, we are most real, Private. And now the matter of our prisoners…" He motioned to the even more haggard-looking Hessians.

"Yes sir, forgive me…"

"Private, you look… unwell," Captain Braxton said, as an idea took shape.

"I... excuse me sir, but I've been sick. I believe I have a fever, sir."

"Yes, you look quite terrible. Frightful, in fact. Go and get some sleep, Private. Fitzsimmons, stand guard here! And the rest of you, we'll take these prisoners to the brig. Private, you are relieved..."

"Yes sir, Captain sir!"

And Malcolm Turner was in the middle of one of the most joyous salutes of his military career when from out of nowhere came a huge dark shape, hard to distinguish in the driving rain. It struck like a rabid wild animal at the middle of Braxton's squad of men, and it was so fast that it seemed to strike everywhere at once and move in a blur. Shots were fired in every direction, but in seconds men were crying out in agony as several fell dead in the mud, the cold rain following them down.

"What in God's name?" Braxton cried out, as he brought out his pistol and fired.

"What the HELL?" yelled Private John Wiley as what looked like a large wolf leapt through the air and tore out his throat.

By now the men were fleeing in all directions, their guns thrown in the air as the beast cut them down one after the next, the last being Private Mandalay Fitzsimmons, leaving Captain Ballistar Braxton standing in the rain as he tossed his pistol to the ground and drew his sword. And the beast stood there, its eyes red as cinders as it gazed upon him, as the rain beat down against its hairy back.

"Come on, hellhound!" Braxton said, making ready with his blade.

And when the creature charged he struck it in the shoulder. But before he could turn around, the monster had taken his other arm in its mouth and snapped it right off as if it were timber. And Captain Braxton staggered for a moment, watching the blood spurt from the end of his missing limb. And when he turned his head, the beast came crashing into his chest. Braxton landed in the mud with the beast on top of him. And he watched in a kind of awestruck horror as it ripped out his heart.

And through it all, Private Mal Turner had slumped to the soggy ground overcome by his illness, to witness the whole gruesome spectacle with eyes half-closed, delirious with fever. And when the blood-soaked creature came over to him it looked at this man and perhaps sensed his disease, as it sniffed once and then turned away and ran off into the forest.

13 March 1778
3 am
Mount Vernon
Virginia

Martha Washington woke from a fitful sleep to what she thought was the growl of a wild animal. She turned in bed looking for her husband but then she realized that this was Mount Vernon; that he was still in Pennsylvania at Valley Forge. The full moon shone through the window. And as she turned her head back to the room she was shocked to see a small boy standing on top of the bed at her feet.

"Mommy," the boy said, "there's something in my room."

Speechless, she took in a breath, her heart pounding beneath her nightgown.

"Mommy," the boy said again, "I'm scared."

But Martha was childless, yet she tried to speak to this child, to offer words of comfort, when suddenly his face changed. His eyes went black and fangs appeared as he opened his mouth. Martha gasped as she heard him growl, right before he lunged across the bed.

When she awoke in a cold sweat she could barely catch her breath, her mouth bone dry, her hands before her throat as if to fend off a wild beast.

13 March 1778
10 am
Valley Forge

That morning the camp was rife with speculation as to what had happened in the early morning hours by the woods near Mount Misery. Men slaughtered. A British raiding party? An attack by rabid wolves? And the most outlandish so far: ghosts from beyond the grave come back to exact vengeance. The soldier's life is a superstitious one to begin with, but today no one did anything without first saying a prayer. Even General Washington was puzzled as to what actually had taken place.

"So men were killed, is that correct Colonel Burr?"

"Yes General, we believe so."

"You believe so?"

"Well, the bodies were so badly mangled. But they were men's bodies, of that we're sure."

For a moment Washington stood nonplused.

"So, in your opinion Colonel, what could have caused such an act of brutality?"

"They're saying wolves, General. A pack of rabid wolves."

"Who is saying that, Colonel?"

"Well, the men, sir. The fact is that no one has ever seen anything like this."

"And the... the unlucky souls... were they British soldiers?"

"No. They appear, from what evidence remains, to be Rebels, sir. Continental soldiers with several men who appear to have been Hessians."

"Hessians?"

"Yes. It appears that a detachment of men arrived in the early morning hours with several Hessians... Hessian prisoners that they had captured when... when the incident occurred, General."

"Do you know who ordered this detachment?"

"No sir, I do not."

Burr was silent for a moment before he spoke again.

"There was a witness, sir."

"A survivor?"

"Yes. But he has been uncommunicative."

"Uncommunicative?"

"He's in the infirmary, sir."

"Was he wounded?"

"No, oddly he was spared. But he's sick with fever. Delusional, sir."

"Did he... did he *say* anything?"

"He said it was a wolf, sir."

"A wolf? A single wolf?"

"That's what he said, sir. But as I said, he was delirious."

"Hmm..." Washington let out a breath. "Well, take me to the spot, Colonel."

"As you wish, General."

Five minutes later they stood in the mud before the scene of slaughter.

"This is Major Seth Grahame-Smith," Colonel Burr explained. "He was the first to... to arrive here, to see..."

"Major..."

"General..."

"So Major, your thoughts..." said General Washington.

"Sir, I... I never saw anything like it in my life, General. I don't know who could even imagine such a thing!"

"My question, Major, was designed to ascertain if you had any knowledge of the parties responsible for... for this..." He looked down at the mutilated bodies.

"Yes sir. I mean no sir," said Major Grahame-Smith. "Thank God for the rain though!"

"Major?"

"The rain, sir... it washed away the blood. What a gruesome mess it must have been!"

"Thank you, Major. You are dismissed."

"Yes sir, General."

And now Washington turned to Aaron Burr.

"They do appear to be our soldiers, don't they?"

"Yes sir."

"And you say there was a witness?"

"Yes sir. A sentry was placed right there, sir." Burr motioned with his hand. "And the... the victims appear to have come from the woods over there." There was a pause. "Whatever it was that attacked them..."

"Colonel Burr..."

"Well sir, like the Major said, the rain washed away all the tracks and left just a muddy mess."

"Hmm," Washington sighed. "Well, have some men take care of... the bodies."

"Right away sir."

At this Baron Von Steuben rode up on his dappled mare.

"Colonel Burr... General Washington..."

And as Von Steuben raised his arm in salute, for a moment he winced.

"Something wrong, Baron?" Washington asked.

"My arm is a little stiff, General. From sleeping on the cold mattress." He looked over at the bodies. "A terrible thing, this. I heard it was a pack of wolves."

"That's what we believe," said Colonel Burr.

Von Steuben nodded and then looked at General Washington, hoping to divine his thoughts.

"I think I'll pay a visit to that sentry who was here," the General said, and then to Burr, "What was his name?"

"Um, I have it right here, sir…" Aaron Burr brought out a pad on which he had scribbled the name. "Private Malcolm Turner, sir."

"Private Malcolm Turner…" George Washington said as he turned from the two officers and rode off towards the infirmary.

13 March 1778
11 am
Valley Forge Infirmary

"General Washington!" Dr. Benjamin Rush exclaimed.

George Washington looked around at all the sick and dying soldiers, the ravages of this winter of deprivation, and he felt indescribably sad.

"So many men…" he let out a sigh.

"Frostbite… pneumonia… high fever… malnutrition…"

"Hmm…"

"So General, to what do I owe the pleasure?"

"Ben, you have a Private Turner here, is that correct?"

"Yes General."

"Can he speak?"

"Well, I'll let you see for yourself." And he led Washington to Turner's cot.

"Private Turner…" Washington began.

"Maaaal…"

"What?"

"He's quite ill, General," said Dr. Rush. "He's been in and out of consciousness."

"Private Turner, can you hear me?"

At that moment Mal Turner opened his eyes and saw General George Washington standing above his bed.

"General Wa… Sir!"

"Easy soldier…" Washington glanced at the doctor and then looked back at Private Turner. "Can you tell me what happened last night?"

"Last night, sir?"

"The attack…"

"You mean the wolf sir?"

"The wolf?"

"That killed Captain Braxton."

"Captain Braxton?" Washington looked to Dr. Rush.

"That's the first he's mentioned a Captain Braxton, General."

"Private Turner, are you sure it was just one wolf?"

"One wolf, sir?"

"That killed Captain Braxton…"

"Von Steuben…"

At this, Washington felt his heart skip a beat.

"What did you say?"

"Under the direct orders of the Inspector General we have four Hessian soldiers as our prisoners…"

"As I said, he's been more or less delirious, sir," said the doctor.

"DAMN ALL… OFFICERS AND… GENTLEMEN!"

Washington smiled to himself as he leaned over the bed.

"Private, can you tell me anything more about Captain Braxton?"

"Captain who?"

"From last night…"

"You look quite terrible… Frightful, in fact…"

"Private?"

"Private, you are relieved…" Mal Turner said, and then he said it again, "Private, you are re-leeeved…"

"He has a high fever, General. He doesn't know what he's saying."

"So I gather. So if he becomes coherent let me know immediately, all right Doctor?"

"Yes General, I will."

"Private, you are RELEEEVED!" the General heard again as he left the infirmary.

When Washington returned to the camp proper he found Colonel Burr and he had him check all the rosters for a Captain Braxton. Burr later reported that there was no officer by that name in the Continental Army.

13 March 1778
2 pm
Valley Forge

Aaron Burr did not like to not know things. At Princeton he had been first in his class, and he always seemed to grasp things before anyone else. But now with the bizarre events of the past few days he was at a loss as to what was going on. The only thing he knew for sure was that it most likely had nothing to do with the British, but rather something that his academic and military training had left him ill-equipped to face.

Burr decided to return to the scene of the slaughter to see if he had missed a crucial piece of evidence. Upon arrival, two enlisted men came up to him with a third man, his hands bound in hemp behind his back.

"Colonel Burr, sir, we've brought back a traitorous deserter for General Washington to dispose of."

"What's your name, soldier?"

"Private David Metz, sir, and this is Private Ophie Kier!"

"Not *your* names, idiots! I mean the deserter's…"

"You heard the Colonel! Speak, traitor!" Private Metz shouted, with an added punch to the ribs for good measure.

"Private Jonathan James, sir."

"Well, Private James, I'm in an exceedingly bad mood. So what do you have to say for yourself?"

"Nothing, sir. I just… I just wanted to go home."

"Ha! Don't you think *I* want to go home as well?"

The deserter was silent.

"Shall we bring him to General Washington?" Private Metz asked.

"What? No, sirrah! The General has enough on his mind without being bothered by you imbeciles!"

"So what shall we do with him, sir?"

Burr thought for a moment.

"Hold him up…" he said.

"Sir?"

"Hold him up straight," he said again.

"You heard him!" said Private Metz to Private Kier.

And when he was propped up between the two, Colonel Burr drew his pistol from its holster, cocked the hammer, and fired, sending pieces of the deserter's bloody brain through the air. And for a moment the two privates stood there with mouths agape, as they still held onto the soldier's lifeless body.

"Get rid of that traitor," Colonel Burr said, "and don't bother me again."

13 March 1778
6:30 pm
Valley Forge
The second night of the full moon

The moon was due to rise at seven pm, but this information was irrelevant to General George Washington as he sat on his gray stallion called Nelson, looking out at the camp. He had been troubled all day with what happened the night before, the butchered troops. And now it was still unknown as to who they were and who (or what) was responsible. And as he surveyed the camp he saw Otto, Van Steuben's dog-hating dwarf, walking briskly towards his small private hut, where he stayed when he wasn't attending to the Baron. Washington remembered what that Private had said about Van Steuben. And although he was obviously raving with fever there was still something about it that bothered the General. And he wheeled his horse around and moved at a trot towards the woods, which led to Van Steuben's quarters.

Colonel Aaron Burr had been troubled as well, but for different reasons. He kept thinking of that cage in the Baron's hut, and that little bastard dwarf who threatened to blow his head off. Burr waited until the dwarf went back to camp before he made his way through the forest. The path was a swath cut through the trees made by the enlisted men several months before, and it now served as a direct route to the Baron's hut. When Burr arrived he saw the owl again, perched ominously on a branch, its strange face with an expression both quizzical and deeply disturbing. Aaron Burr was convinced that if he ever went to Hell this creature would greet him upon his arrival. He reached for his pistol but then he noticed that tonight there was a padlock on the door outside. He sighed to himself that he had only one bullet in his pistol and he wasn't in the mood to reload. So he turned and aimed his weapon at the lock on the door. The report of his flintlock echoed through the woods as the owl took wing. Burr removed the shattered padlock and put his hand to the doorknob when a sharp voice pierced the air.

"Colonel Burr, what are you doing?"

It was General Washington astride his horse, his saber at his side.

"General Washington! I... You startled me, sir!"

"Yes, but I asked you what you were doing."

"I was... I was checking on the Inspector General, sir, I... I heard a gunshot."

Washington looked down at the padlock on the ground and then at Burr's sidearm as the young Colonel remained silent.

"Get back to camp, Colonel Burr... at once."

"Yes General."

Washington waited until Burr and his horse had disappeared from view before he dismounted. Walking over he picked up the padlock. It was destroyed from where it had been struck by the bullet, and then the General turned to the hut. Quietly he opened the door and stepped inside.

"Otto, is that you?" came a voice from the darkness. "I heard a gunshot..."

The only light shone in through the open door, and what Washington saw made him catch his breath. Before him was a huge cage taking up almost the entire room and in it was Baron Von Steuben, standing naked in the shadows.

"Baron! What happened? Who *did* this to you?"

"General, you must leave here immediately. There's not much time..."

"What? What are you talking about?"

Washington rushed to the cage and found that it was locked.

"Who did this? Was it your dwarf?"

"You must leave here at once, General! Before it's too late!"

"Where's the key, Baron?" Washington shook the door, but the cage was formidable.

"General, you must..."

"Baron, where's the key?"

"You must go at once!" implored Von Steuben. "Otherwise..."

Washington stood there, unable to comprehend. Stepping closer he looked at the Baron's face. It was gripped by some kind of inner torment, his features transformed into a look of such sadness as if his very soul had been lost.

"Baron, I have to get you out of there. Stand back!" Washington brought out his pistol and aimed it at the lock.

"NO! PLEASE!" Von Steuben's voice strained. "GET OUT NOW!"

And then the Baron saw the familiar change in the light shining through the open door. The moon had begun to rise.

"It's too late..." Von Steuben said.

And George Washington looked into his eyes and was moved by a kind of inner agony that overcame them, and he stood before the cage transfixed.

1738
A forest in East Prussia

The only sound was the fire, the flames gently consuming the logs with the occasional pop as a spark shot out, but to the boy sitting before the hearth these were cannonballs bursting in air. Young Friedrich sat before a great army. Painted metal soldiers in Prussian battle dress, with shouldered muskets and a phalanx of cannon aimed at the Swedish troops. The Great Northern War which lasted for twenty-one years was being fought here tonight on the rough wooden floor, eight year-old Freddy von Steuben in command as General of all Prussian forces. And in the chair across the room sat his father, Wilhelm Augustin, with his pipe, his face aglow in candlelight as he watched his only son. His wife Elizabeth had died in childbirth eight years before, and since then he would be the first to admit that he indulged his only child. It was far too late, well past Freddy's bedtime. Yet it was so peaceful sitting there before the fire on this long winter's night, watching his son fight for Prussian independence. And the thing that his father marveled at was that it was all done in silence. The soldiers maneuvered across the field, the cannon were fired, the men fell to the ground in agonized death, but it all took place within young Friedrich's mind where the cannon, the gunshots, the screams of the wounded were deafening.

Wilhelm Augustin took a puff from his pipe as he watched his son execute a left oblique, which put the Swedish regiment in enfilade. And he smiled as young Freddy brought his cannon to bear. If his son had been in command the Great Northern War might not have lasted twenty-one years, he smiled to himself. And then he noticed the fire. More logs were needed if they were to stay warm through the night, and there was only one left in the pile.

"I have to get more wood," he said to his son.

"Yes father."

"But when I return it's your bedtime."

"Yes father," Freddy nodded. And then he issued the command to charge as his father went outside.

Minutes later, out of the stillness of mid-winter came an unearthly cry, like the howl of a wolf, but something more. Freddy hurried to the window and looked out. He saw his father standing before the woodshed, his arms filled with logs, his eyes staring off into the forest. And then from the shadows it came. It was so fast his father still held the wood when he was attacked, and Friedrich watched as the beast knocked him down and proceeded to tear him apart. Horrified, Friedrich pressed his little face against the window, the thick glass making everything wavy outside, making the scene itself like something from a dream or a nightmare. His father's screaming went on as Friedrich was powerless to move, almost enraptured by what was happening. The beast was so powerful, its jaws ripped apart flesh with ease. In moments the snow was covered in a dark stain that looked black beneath the moonlight. And when it was over Friedrich uttered a single word, "Father..." as he wiped the glass with his hand. And then to his shock he saw the monster turn and face the house, the window, as if it could see him standing there. Immediately the boy took a breath and staggered backwards. Behind him was the whole Prussian Army, but Freddy's eyes were fixed on the window. And a moment later he saw two eyes, like red coals peering in, and the young boy stood paralyzed as though he had died and was turned to stone. Time was erased as this moment went on, as the beast tilted its head and gazed inside, at this boy, at the fire. And Friedrich Von Steuben stood there inert, his hands shaking uncontrollably. It was a moment beyond thought, beyond hope when all one feels is fear. The werewolf's nose pressed against the window now, its breath fogged up the glass. Any second now it will crash inside, and Friedrich closed his eyes as his last conscious act and waited. Minutes went by; an hour perhaps, when suddenly the boy opened his eyes as if released from a spell. There was nothing outside. The beast was gone. Friedrich turned and looked at the hearth. The fire had died, and he fell to the floor by the embers, curling into himself until morning.

At first light he saw the metal soldiers, some of them still in formation. And then he looked to his father's chair. It was empty, his pipe in its bowl on the small table beside it.

"Father?" he said. "Father?"

He walked to his father's room. The door was opened and the bed was still made. And then he remembered the window and he went outside. An overcast morning, still very cold. There were footsteps in the snow of some kind of animal. And then he saw his father—his father's remains, that is—in the snow by the woodshed, the blood dark red in the early morning light.

"So it had happened..." he said to himself, so quietly that not even God could hear.

1750
Midsummer
East Prussia

The horse was black, its hide slick with sweat. Its rider had run him hard. And then she saw its rider. A young man, a soldier in the King's Army. His body was strong, his face pleasing to the eye. But a look of sadness was there as well, as if he had seen things, terrible things in the span of this young life.

"If I may be so bold as to request some water for my horse… and for myself," he said, still in the saddle.

And as she looked up at him their worlds seemed so far apart. Her world: the earth, the animals, milking cows, and churning butter. His world: the world of men and weapons and great conquering armies. And he seemed to float above her now like some young god of war.

"So, the water…" he said.

"Yes!"

"You are very kind."

"And you are quite the gentleman, young sir."

"Well, I've been accused of many things…" he smiled. "May I have your permission to dismount?"

"Ha," she smiled. "Yes you may."

Standing before her he seemed even more splendid, with his well-polished riding boots, his tight breeches, his tailored uniform, and she did her best, being a young maiden of virtue, to conceal her obvious delight.

"Allow me to introduce myself," he said, taking off his hat and sweeping it in a grand gesture through the air. "I am Baron Friedrich Wilhelm Augustin Ludolf Gerhard Von Steuben, Captain and member of the General Staff of his Majesty Frederick the Great the King of All Prussia."

"Hmm," she said. "I'm Lil."

"Lil?"

"It's short for Lily."

"Of course it is!" he smiled. "What a lovely name!"

"And yours…"

"Ha," he laughed. "Could I have been more pompous?"

"I don't know," she replied. "I don't know what that means… pompous."

"So much the better if none of us knew!" he said. "Perhaps I should begin again. Allow me to introduce myself… I am Freddy."

"Freddy. I'm delighted to meet you!"

"And I you, Lily."

"Lil."

"Yes, Lil. So are you making butter?" he motioned to the churn by her side.

"Yes, would you like some?"

"Well, I was hoping to get some water for myself and for my horse. We've had a long journey."

"Yes, I'm sorry! There's the trough for your mount, but as for you, kind sir, I beg you to be patient a moment longer."

"I am at your disposal, Lil," he executed a deep bow.

Several minutes passed, and then the young woman returned with a glass of ice cold water which she handed to him.

"Mmm, this is delicious! From the river!"

"The river?" she looked shocked. "How do you know about the river?"

"It's just through those trees," he smiled.

He saw the puzzled look on her face. And what a lovely face it was. So unlike the girls of Brandenburg and Berlin, with their fancy dress, their painted faces, their city intrigues.

"Forgive me," he said. "Many years ago as a small boy I used to live right here, in this very house that you live in now."

"What? Really?"

"Yes. I was eight years old the last time I saw *any* of this…"

For a moment Lil was speechless.

"I left for the city shortly after my eighth birthday, to Magdeburg to live with my Uncle, to be trained in the military arts."

"I have heard of Magdeburg. Is it a great and beautiful city?"

"It is a city, like all cities…"

"Hmm?"

"It is overcrowded with everything, I'm afraid. That's why I wanted to come back here, to see if it was still the same."

"Well, is it?"

"Yes, mostly… but with some surprises."

At this she smiled softly.

"So Lil, how long have you lived here, in these woods?"

"We came here ten years ago. This house was in great disrepair, having been abandoned."

"But you've fixed it up so nicely. It looks better than it did."

"It's my father. He's a carpenter. He's in the forest right now cutting wood."

"And your mother?"

"She died of fever last winter."

"I'm so sorry."

"Thank you."

At that, two small boys appeared chasing each other, holding sticks and making the sounds of musket fire.

"These are my two horrible brothers," Lil explained. "Caspar and Karlheinz, but we call him Karl…"

Upon seeing the young officer in uniform the two boys snapped to attention and brought their little hands to their foreheads in salute.

"Dismissed…" Freddy said.

"Why don't you go off and play?" Lil said, eager to be alone again with the handsome young officer. And at her urging the boys ran off. "Would you like some more water?"

"No thank you."

"May I ask what you are doing here, young sir?"

"Yes, forgive me. I… I came to see *this!*" he said. "Your house which used to be my own. I am on a two week furlough and… I've often thought about this place, about when I lived here. I assure you I mean no harm. My plan was to come here, see the house, then stay in town for a few days at the Inn. I hope I haven't been too much of a bother."

"No, of course not. It has been my pleasure."

"Can I ask you something though, Lil?"

"Yes, what is it?"

"These woods, do you… do you like living so close to them, in the middle of them in fact? So far away from… well, civilization?"

"Why yes," she laughed. "What an odd question."

"Forgive me, I…"

"No, it's all right. So can I ask *you* something, Baron?"

"Freddy."

"Yes, Freddy… Now I am asking this on behalf of my father, so you won't think me untoward…"

"No, I… I would never think that."

"Good, I'm glad. So I would like to invite you…"

"On behalf of your father…"

"On behalf of my father, to join us for supper tonight…"

"It… It would be my honor." Freddy bowed gallantly.

"I am so pleased," said Lil. "Then I will see you back here at six o'clock… after I've had the chance to tell my father all about you."

"Well that shouldn't take too long."

"You are too modest," she said. "Your title alone…"

"Hmm… Forgive me, I…"

"I'm teasing," she smiled.

"Are you sure?"

"Yes!" And she reached out and shook his hand. "Until this evening then?"

"Until this evening."

At dinner that night Lil's father couldn't have been more pleased, to have a Captain in Frederick the Great's Army right there in his home!

"So, my daughter tells me that you are on the General Staff of King Frederick…"

"Yes, I am."

"So have you… I mean, surely you must have…"

"Met the King? Yes, many times. I discuss with him military strategy and tactics."

"Do you? At such a young age…"

"I am twenty, sir."

"Ah, when you say it it sounds very old. My daughter however is still only sixteen."

"Daddy, please…"

"What? Is it my fault I love my daughter? That I'm protective? That I'm proud of her?"

"But I don't do *anything*, Daddy, I…"

"On the contrary," said Freddy. "You make the most delicious butter that I've ever tasted!"

"Really?"

"Not in Berlin or Magdeburg have I tasted any as sweet."

"We hope you will dine with us each night," her father said, "for the duration of your stay."

"Nothing, sir, would give me greater pleasure."

"Good. So it's settled."

And suddenly more seemed to be going on than just plans for dinner.

That night after everyone had gone to bed, Lil stood outside with Freddy beneath the waxing moon.

"I love the summer nights," she said. "Especially in the moonlight. Everything is so bright, like daytime."

"The moon will be full in three days," Freddy said.

"Oh I so wish that you will stay until then."

"But I used to live here, you remember? I've seen it before."

"But not…"

She was going to say, "But not with me," but decorum held her tongue. And as if sensing this, Freddy reached over and gently touched her hand.

"Yes," he said. "In fact, I want nothing more than to spend every minute with you as long as my stay allows."

"Me too," she smiled.

And in the thrall of this burgeoning romance the days flew by. And by the third day, as was the custom, Friedrich had proposed and Lil had accepted. Her father planned a celebratory dinner at the house that evening, Friedrich arriving in full dress uniform, his saber at his side. But all this was interrupted when Caspar came home in tears.

"What happened?" his father asked. "Where's Karl?"

"He… we were climbing trees and he fell!"

"In the woods?"

"Yes, I… I think he broke his leg! I'm so sorry, Papa!"

And at that moment Friedrich's heart leapt into his throat and he could barely breathe.

"How far?" his father asked.

"Past the pond."

"Past the *pond?* That'll take at least an hour there and back. And it's almost dark."

"I'm sorry, Papa!" Caspar said again, and then the tears came.

"Hmm," his father sighed. "Don't worry, it's not your fault," he patted the boy's head. "Well, I better get going."

And he walked to the mantle and grabbed the musket from the wall as Friedrich thought of the moon. Tonight it would be full.

"Let *me* go," Friedrich said.

"What?"

"Freddy!" said Lil.

"I insist. Let me go in your place, sir, and I will find your son."

"But we can go together," the old man offered.

"No!" And there was a pause as the two men looked at each other. "Please," Friedrich said in a softer tone now, "you've been so kind. Please allow me to repay your kindness."

The old man considered it for a moment and then nodded his head.

"Then I accept," he said, "as I welcome in spirit my new son."

"Thank you. And I my new father... But, may I borrow your weapon?" he motioned to the musket.

"Yes of course! But how will you... how will you find the pond? The woods are so dark."

"You forget, I lived here as a boy," Friedrich smiled. "I used to play in these woods all the time."

The old man nodded in assent, and minutes later Friedrich walked back into the forest, this place he had thought about and dreaded for the past twelve years. Daylight was fading fast and beneath the dense trees it was almost night. After awhile he wondered if he could remember how to get there, to the pond (it had been so long) when suddenly he heard branches snap behind him. Cocking the gun he pointed it into darkness when he heard a voice.

"Freddy? Freddy?"

"Lil?" He couldn't have been more surprised. "What are you doing here?" he asked. "Why? Why did you come?"

"To show you the way," she laughed. "It's very dark."

"No! No! You... You have to go back *immediately!* You... I insist!" And he looked around at the trees, so menacing, so unwelcoming.

"But then you'll be lost as well as my brother," she said, "and I'll go out of my mind waiting and I'll just end up coming here anyway to search for you."

Friedrich saw the look on her face, that she was not to be dissuaded, and he let out a long deep breath.

"All right," he said, "but I want you to stay close to me at all times, do you hear?"

"Yes sir, Baron Von Steuben, sir!"

The night came down quickly and soon the only light was from the moon ripping through the trees, its light slashing the branches. Friedrich remembered the feeling of when he was eight: of looking out the window; of the horrible sounds; of his heart about to explode; of the cold sweat covering his skin; of being so scared that he had tried to convince himself over the past twelve years that it had never happened; that it was a nightmare he had once as a child, before his father left him without a word.

"The pond is just up ahead," Lil whispered.

And as they came to a clearing they saw the water illuminated, the reflection of the moon on its surface. And then at the edge of the pond what looked like a large animal drinking from the water's edge.

"What's that?" Lil asked, but Friedrich knew all too well.

"Ssssh!" he said. "We have to go back!"

"What? But what about Karl?"

And right then the animal turned its head and stared at them both.

"Is that a wolf?" she asked.

But it was too late. Before they could move the werewolf attacked. Friedrich got off a shot but it had no effect, and the creature struck the side of Lil's body ripping apart her chest. And then it came at him and he hit it with the butt end of the rifle releasing a hideous scream. The beast appeared in a pool of moonlight now, its bullet wound dripping blood but murder still in its eyes. And as it prepared to charge, Friedrich withdrew his sword. The beast lunged for his throat and he wheeled and swung the saber as the creature rushed past. Another cry as the blade tore through its shoulder. And as it reared again and leapt through the air, Friedrich swung his sword in a single arc that severed the beast's head and left it before him on the ground. The monster was dead, but to make sure he kicked its head into the pond and watched as it sank. He then went over to Lil, to her body. He had seen this before. Her eyes were still opened, frozen in this terrified expression of death.

"Lil..." he said softly. "Lil..."

He had known her for less than a week but he loved her more than he had loved anyone. And there she was, dead on the ground, on the fresh summer grass next to some evening primrose whose flowers bloom in the moonlight. And then he noticed the blood dripping from his hand, the gash on his arm. He had been bitten.

An hour later Lil's father wept over her dead body, as Friedrich had carried it back for burial. And in the morning they went back into the woods. They found the decapitated body of the werewolf, although now it was nothing more than a man.

"Where is the head?" the old man asked.

"There…" Friedrich said, "at the bottom of the pond."

"That's a shame," he said. "I would like to have known who killed my daughter.

"I… I'm sorry."

The old man looked past him at some dry brush, and a short time later he had made a fire in which to burn the headless man's body. And while they looked for more wood so that the fire would burn hot, Friedrich discovered what was left of Karl amidst some fallen limbs. Karl was only eight, the same age he had been. They waited before the fire for a long time, until only ashes remained, and then they brought Karl's body back home. And after the two children were buried their father said a prayer.

"May the Lord take you both and give you the peace that was stolen from you in this life…" And then he turned to Friedrich. "You must go now," he said, "and never return. The moon will be full again tonight and you'll become like that creature… that thing that murdered my daughter, that murdered my son."

"What are you talking about?" Friedrich asked.

"You've been bitten," said the old man. "You'll change." And there was a pause as he looked at the three graves side by side, the third belonging to his wife. "I should kill you now," he said, "before it happens. The forest had been peaceful all the years we lived here but somehow you… I don't know, you've awakened some kind of evil!" He looked at the musket atop the woodpile and took a deep breath. "But because you loved my daughter and because she loved you I can't kill you. No… But you must go. You must be far away from here, far away from *anyone* before the moon rises. Do you understand?"

"No, I…"

"Well you *must!*" the old man insisted. "You must! So go now, please, and never come back."

13 March 1778
7:01 pm
Valley Forge
The second night of the full moon

All this passed through Friedrich Von Steuben's head as he felt the change coming on, as it had every month for the past twenty-eight years. And he looked into George Washington's eyes and hoped with all his soul (if he still had one) to spare him from such a fate.

"Please, General… you must go," he said in a voice so weak now as to barely be heard.

And Washington looked on, still not comprehending. Von Steuben gripped the bars of the cage and started to shake as if in the grip of some uncontrollable spasm.

"Please… go…" Von Steuben pleaded. "PLEASE…"

And then there was the terrible sound of bones cracking, of muscles tearing, of the Baron moaning in agony as fur grew from his skin, claws from his fingers, fangs from his teeth; as his entire body convulsed and distorted and his face became that of a wolf. George Washington watched in horror as the transformation became complete, and what stood before him now was not a man and not a beast but an Abomination. Something evil and wretched.

Something to be pitied and to be put out of its misery. And Washington drew his pistol and took aim, but stopped for a moment as he looked into the monster's eyes. They were red and cold and devoid of all humanity and only reflected the soul at its most base and depraved. And Washington extended his arm and fired. The bullet hit the beast square in the forehead, but instead of falling back it lunged forward and grabbed the General's arm through the iron bars, pulling him close. George Washington felt its claws tear through his clothing, rake across his skin, its terrible jaws snapping the air, ripping out pieces of flesh, *his* flesh. And it was all he could do to wrest himself free as he fell against the wall of the hut and collapsed to the floor.

14 March 1778
6 am
Von Steuben's hut

It was morning when George Washington awoke, finding himself on the cold wooden floor covered in his own blood. Being a soldier, the first thing he did was to ascertain the extent of his wounds. There were several deep gashes in his chest and what looked like bite marks on his arm. But they all seemed to be healing. The bleeding had stopped. And then he looked over at the cage and saw Friedrich Von Steuben standing naked against the bars.

"I'm deeply sorry, General," the Baron said.

"What happened?" Washington tried to get to his feet but suddenly grew dizzy.

"Don't try to stand up, sir."

"But I don't understand… My head, I…"

"Headache?"

"Yes."

"It's the first sign."

"The first sign of what?"

"Of the change…"

"The change? What are you talking about? What happened here? What… What happened to me?" he motioned to his wounds.

"Don't you remember?"

"No, I..."

"You were attacked, General..."

"Attacked? By whom?"

"By what..."

"By what?"

"You were attacked by a werewolf."

"A were..."

And then he began to remember. George Washington sat back against the wall and closed his eyes, and he could see it all in his memory as if it had just taken place. When he opened his eyes again he stared at Von Steuben for a long time without speaking, as it continued to sink in.

"You... so you are..."

"Yes, General... I'm so sorry, I... I tried to warn you..."

"But, how... How can it *be*? How can..."

"I don't know. Who *knows* what terrible things God allows to exist?" said Von Steuben. "I only know that some things do."

At that moment Otto appeared, frantic, his flintlock drawn and aimed at General Washington's head. The dwarf cocked the hammer and was about to fire when the Baron intervened.

"No, Otto! No!"

"But sir..."

"I said no. I'm fine, Otto. Now leave us, please. The General and I have some things to discuss..."

"Are you sure?"

"Yes, Otto. Thank you."

Otto nodded and turned to leave.

"But first..." Von Steuben motioned to the lock on the cage. "The key, Otto... if you would be so kind..."

And the dwarf brought the key from his waistcoat pocket and unlocked the cage.

"Thank you, Otto. We will have much to talk about later, you and I. But for now I'm sure General Washington has some burning questions for me."

"I understand, sir," and Otto left the hut and closed the door.

"Would you mind terribly if I put on some clothes?" Von Steuben asked.

"No, of course not," Washington replied. "I still... I still can't..."

"Believe it?"

"Yes."

"Hmm."

"I mean, we hear stories of demons, of vampires and werewolves but..."

"They're stories and nothing more..."

"Yes," Washington nodded.

"I was eight years old," Von Steuben began. "My father went outside to get wood for the fire. It was the night of a full moon and I watched from the window as... as my father was butchered without mercy. And for twelve years I thought... I *believed* that I had imagined it, you know? That it was some young boy's nightmare, for how could it be otherwise?"

"So... when did *you*..."

"I was twenty. A young officer... a Captain in the Prussian Army... My fiancée, a beautiful young woman was... was attacked and murdered by a beast, and I was bitten like you and like you I survived," he laughed bitterly.

"And it was a werewolf?"

"What else? And I became one as well..."

"But..."

"No General, there are no buts... it's what the French call a *fait accompli*. You've been bitten, General... I'm so sorry. And especially that it was myself who did it. I know this is something that's... well, unforgivable. But at least I can tell you a few things to... well, to help you... accept it."

"Accept it? How? How in God's name am I to do such a thing, Baron, if what you say is true?"

"It *is* true, General. Next month when the moon is full you'll change exactly as I did last night. You saw what happened. You saw what I became..."

Washington took a breath.

"But... there must be... there must be a..."

"A cure?" Von Steuben laughed. "The only cure is death, I'm afraid."

"But, I mean I *shot* you!" Washington insisted. "Last night! In the head at point blank range!"

"The beast, for whatever unholy reason, cannot be killed by bullets or knives..." Von Steuben explained.

"But when you were bitten, what happened to... to *it?*"

"I cut off its head with my sword. The beast may be killed by decapitation, and then its head must be separated from its body and the body burned. This is the only way I know of to kill it."

"Other than..."

"Other than..."

"Well, suicide..."

"Suicide, yes... You have no idea how this has occupied my thoughts over the past twenty-eight years..."

"So, I mean why *didn't* you, dammit?" Washington stood up now, irate. "Those men in the woods the other night... that was *you!*"

The Baron nodded.

"How? How in God's name? How can you... murder people like that? Innocent people! How can... How can you *live* with yourself after doing such things?"

"I can't!" Von Steuben said. "But I've found to my everlasting shame that I can't kill myself either. I'm... I'm weak, General Washington. I've killed countless men in battle without batting an eye, men who were my enemy, but... I don't have the... the courage to do this thing that must be done. And I stand before you now not fit to see the sun, to breathe the air. In fact, would you do me the honor, General Washington?"

"Baron?"

"Take my pistol, sir..." The Baron handed Washington his weapon. "Do it, General. Please..."

And George Washington stood there with gun in hand as he stared at Von Steuben.

"I can't take it any longer, General. Please!"

Washington cocked the hammer and raised his arm, the gun pointed at the same spot on the Baron's forehead.

"DO IT!" Von Steuben demanded. "DO IT!"

"I... I *CAN'T!*" Washington said. "I can't..." And he shook his head and put the gun aside.

Von Steuben nodded in resignation.

"Then there are things I must tell you," he began. "Things you will need to know..."

"But, I mean if you have this cage why do you still..."

"You will find as the days of the month wear on, as it gets closer to the full moon you will get terrible headaches, muscle aches, gut-wrenching pain so severe as to be almost unbearable. In fact you'll feel as if you are about to die. But of course you won't. You'll just suffer horribly until the full moon, and then when you change..."

"What? What happens then?"

The Baron let out a breath.

"Well, at first I... I had no desire to... to be a killer," he said. "To kill innocent people like my father, like... my fiancée. So I locked myself up in the basement during each full moon. I would wait it out, you see! But the pain, it became so great that I could no longer stand it! You have no idea what it will be like, General. Like nothing you've ever felt before. So the day came when I *didn't* lock myself up. And when I changed I... I went out, I killed people, I... I assume that I did, I... I *know* I did," he said. "I just can't remember what happens. I only know that the next day I feel reborn! Indomitable! So strong as if I can do anything!"

"And the pain?" Washington asked.

"The pain is gone!" Von Steuben smiled. "Like magic! And for a while... well, I didn't care, as long as the pain was gone. But then... I found out that I had murdered someone I knew. A close friend, and... Hmm, I couldn't stand the thought. So the following month on the second night of the full moon I kept myself locked in the cage..."

"The *second* night?" said Washington. "What about the *first* night?"

"I know you will find this hard to under..."

"What about the first night, Baron?"

Von Steuben was reluctant to speak.

"The first night I was free," he confessed.

"Free? So you killed?"

"This way the pain…"

"So you killed!" Washington said again.

"This way the pain would subside by my release and…"

"Your release? You make it sound therapeutic! You allowed yourself to murder without consequence!"

"But only for one night not two!"

"One night not two? I can't believe what you're saying!"

"But you *still* don't know what it's like, General! Of not being able to release it, this evil that fills you with its poison until you're ready to explode or… or be destroyed by it! This great and terrible thing that you've become! I *had* to! I had to let myself be free for that one night! It was the only way I could live all the *rest* of the time!"

At this Washington was disgusted and he picked up the gun and pointed it again at the Baron. And then as quickly he turned the gun on himself, he cocked the hammer and pressed its barrel into the side of his head. Von Steuben watched him take a breath, start to move his finger over the trigger, but then he reset the hammer and threw the gun against the wall. And George Washington sank to the floor, hopeless now, his head in his hands.

"So I'll change?" he looked up at Von Steuben, his voice filled with despair.

"Yes, you will. But… I'll help you."

"Help me? What can you do?"

"You need to find a place, General. A place isolated. Something with a basement where you can lock yourself inside when… when it happens."

"Inside a cage…"

"Yes."

"Like an animal…"

"No. You are not an animal, sir, you are…"

"I know, a werewolf."

"Yes."

"But… I don't want to kill anyone," Washington said. "I won't allow myself to do that!"

"I understand, General. That's why it's imperative that you find such a place where you can safely endure the change. And you must have someone whom you trust implicitly to serve as your protector, to lock you in and then release you when the time has passed."

"Like Otto…"

"Yes. Although we didn't expect you to pay me a visit. I underestimated you, sir."

"And now the consequences are my own."

"I'm afraid so."

Washington nodded his head.

"I understand this, Baron, and I realize that it wasn't your fault, what happened with you and… with me. But there's one thing I must ask of you, that I must demand of you…"

"What is it, General?"

"As long as you're here under my command I cannot allow you to… to murder anymore people. Do you understand? You must lock yourself in that cage for *both* nights."

"General, I…"

"I have grown quite fond of you, Baron. I think that we have even become friends, so please do this for me as a personal favor, out of friendship and respect…"

There was a long pause, and then Von Steuben took a deep breath.

"Yes, General," he nodded. "I will do as you ask."

"Thank you, Baron."

And the two men bowed their heads to each other as they felt this strange bond between them.

"So what do we do now?" Washington asked.

"We… We fight the British!" Von Steuben smiled. "We win the war!"

"What? Like none of this ever happened?"

"As far as the world is concerned none of this *did* ever happen. This is to be our secret, General. A secret which I'm afraid we'll take to our deaths."

"And when will that be, Baron? Our deaths?"

"I have no idea, General Washington. I have no idea."

17 March 1778
9 am
Washington's quarters

The days following "the event" were troubling ones for George Washington. Not only did he still have to keep his army together and prepare for the summer campaign, he now had the burden of what he was and what he would become. He took the Baron's advice and commandeered an old stone farmhouse, all by itself in the middle of a cow pasture a mile from camp. And then he engaged a local ironsmith to construct a cage, which was assembled in the basement of his new house, all done *sub rosa*. He explained it was for the interrogation and detainment of prisoners, specifically Hessians (whom everyone detested), so the ironsmith cheerfully obliged. Then there was the matter of finding someone whom he could trust to lock and unlock the basement door during the days and nights of the full moon. Someone who would follow his orders without asking too many questions. Such a man was Alexander Hamilton.

At twenty-three, Hamilton was a Lieutenant Colonel and General Washington's aide-de-camp. So it seemed fitting that like Otto the dwarf, Alexander Hamilton would be the custodian and protector of George Washington's dark and terrible secret.

At first the General was going to tell Hamilton everything, but as the young man sat across from him in his tent the whole thing seemed more and more preposterous.

"General, I... I still don't understand why you wanted to see me."

How to broach the subject? Washington thought. How to phrase it in such a way where he doesn't think me insane?

"General, sir? Are you all right?"

"Yes, I... thank you Colonel, for asking. And the reason I asked you here is to... is to..."

"Sir..."

"It's because I want to commend you for all your hard work and dedication, especially since we've been here, at Valley Forge. I know it's been tough for everyone, but you have been my right hand, my rock on which I have too often leaned."

"Thank you, sir. It has been an honor and a privilege."

"Yes, there's just one more thing..." Washington added.

"Sir?"

"I have recently come into possession of a house... the old Musgrave farmhouse. Do you know it?"

"The Musgrave Farm... it's about a mile from camp, is it not?"

"Yes, that's the place."

"It's rather isolated, sir..."

"Yes it is. I needed a place away from... away from here!" Washington said, improvising like an Italian actor.

"I understand, sir. A place away from the hustle and bustle of the men."

"Exactly!"

"Where you can enjoy some solitude, and where the burden of command may be borne more easily."

"Precisely!"

"And where your mind will be free to envision new stratagems that will precipitate the war's end. And the sooner the better, if I may be so bold as to add, sir."

"You may, and you are exactly to the point as usual, Colonel."

"Thank you, sir. So what do you require of me in this regard?"

"Your discretion, Colonel Hamilton, as this is a matter of the utmost secrecy…"

"Yes, General sir. Of course."

"Good. You are familiar with the Farmer's Almanack?"

"The Farmer's Almanack, sir?" For a moment Hamilton was taken aback. "Yes sir, I am."

"Excellent. So I would like you to consult the Almanack for the days of the month when the moon is full…"

"Sir?"

"And on those days and those days alone you will ride out to the Musgrave farm. Once there your task will be simple, and to you perhaps even meaningless, yet I assure you it is of the utmost importance."

"Yes sir, I am yours to command."

"Very good. So when you are inside the Musgrave house you will find the door to the basement. On the evening of the full moon precisely one hour before the moon is to rise you will lock the basement door and retain the key on your person at all times. And the following morning precisely one hour after dawn you will return to the house and unlock the basement, leaving the key on the nail by the door. And then you will leave and repeat this again until the cycle of the full moon is complete."

"And then what, General?"

"Then you will repeat this exact procedure the next month and every month to follow until I say otherwise. Is that clear, Colonel Hamilton?"

"Absolutely, General Washington, sir!"

Washington was surprised that it had gone so well. He looked at the young officer's face and saw the utmost trust and respect. He had chosen his protector well.

"So, will there be anything else, sir?" Hamilton inquired.

"No, Colonel, that will be all. You are dismissed."

"Yes sir."

And Hamilton offered a crisp salute and then left the tent, being saluted himself by a barefoot Private on the way out who held threadbare shoes in his hand. And what neither he nor George Washington knew was that this Private, one Solomon Bundy, was quite skilled in the art of eavesdropping as he had overheard every word.

But maybe it *was* a dream, Washington thought to himself as he sat alone in his tent. A delusion brought on by stress, fatigue, overwork. After all, it *was* too unbelievable to be true. But then the General pulled up his shirtsleeve. The bite marks were there, healing nicely, but still there.

21 March 1778
9 am
Washington's quarters
Valley Forge

The Vernal Equinox brought with it warm spring weather, and from the muddy earth came blue and purple crocuses, and from the forsythia bushes bright yellow blossoms. And for a few days the camp at Valley Forge was filled with color.

George Washington however likened his own thoughts to the mud that was all around—shapeless, messy, opaque—without any spring flowers in sight. So it was with even more confusion that he agreed to meet with Baron Von Steuben, to discuss "a matter of great military significance". Since "the event" Washington had tried his best to avoid the Baron, but after many entreaties he finally acquiesced.

"General Washington," Von Steuben began, "I am so pleased you agreed to see me. If you don't mind, I'll come right to the point…"

"Please do."

"When I was on the staff of Frederick the Great of Prussia he had his eyes set on Silesia, Frederick that is. But the war did not go as smoothly as he had hoped. And then we realized that we had in our possession a great weapon of war that would make us invincible..."

"And what would that be, Baron?"

Von Steuben smiled. "Our curse, General. Some might say our gift... We created an entire company of werewolves and then we unleashed them on the enemy. And by the time the full moon cycle was complete we had conquered Silesia!"

There was a long awkward silence before Washington finally spoke.

"You want to infect my army? To turn them into these... *creatures* so we can defeat the British?"

"That is precisely what I'm proposing..."

Another pause.

"Thank you, Baron..." Washington said, suddenly feeling light-headed, vertiginous. The world seemed to grow more incomprehensible with each passing day. "Thank you," he said again, and he nodded his head blankly as if that were all to be said.

Baron Von Steuben looked at the General for a moment longer, and then executed a deep courtly bow.

"General..." he said, and he took his leave.

2 April 1778
2 pm
Valley Forge

Ever since the night of his ill-fated guard duty Private Mal Turner had become a pariah among the rest of the men. They figured that since he had somehow survived the bloodbath without a scratch that he must somehow be in league with the Devil. And after he recovered from his illness he received the cold shoulder from everyone in camp. Even his best friend Solomon Bundy kept his distance until finally Mal Turner confronted him.

"Sol!" he called out. "Sol!"

No response.

"I *know* you can hear me!" Mal said, as he ran to catch up with his former friend. "Unless you've suddenly gone deaf!"

At this Bundy turned around.

"I'm not deaf!" he said in a heightened whisper. "But you gotta stay away from me, Mal! They say you're cursed!"

"Not you too, Sol?"

"I'm sorry Mal, but there's no way anyone could have survived that. They say it's the Devil's work."

"But I can't even remember what *happened!*" Mal insisted. "I was so sick, I… I don't even know *what* I saw."

"They say there's a demon on the loose," said Bundy. "Some kind of monster."

"But it's *me,* Sol! Your old friend Mal..."

"I'm sorry," he said. "I'm glad you're feeling better but I can't be seen with you, Mal, it's... bad luck... Sorry." And Solomon Bundy peremptorily turned his back and hurried off.

And Private Malcolm Turner wondered what he had done to deserve such a fate. Last Christmas he was engaged to a lovely young woman, he had good friends and hope for the future. Now he was alone and outcast, as this war dragged on and on as if it would never end.

10 April 1778
11 pm
Nelle Watson's bedroom
The Village of Valley Forge

Aaron Burr did not really care much for Nelle Watson, even as her head was beneath the blankets, bobbing up and down noisily over his prick. She delivered milk to the camp, one of the many young girls who worked as milkmaids for the cause. And at first Burr thought she was rather comely, with her shapely figure and modest demeanor. But she was anything but modest in the bedroom. And since this was all that interested Aaron Burr, for a few weeks she suited him just fine. But now that the bloom was off the rose, or rather that her particular flower had been so many times plucked, even pleasure such as this had become tiresome.

Burr was still frustrated over what became known as "The Massacre". Its cause remained unknown, although the rumors grew wilder and more rampant each day, to the point where there was a palpable unease over the camp. You could see it in every face, right up to General Washington's. Something had happened that had changed everything, although no one seemed to know what it was. And Colonel Aaron Burr was determined to find out.

He looked back at the lump under the covers and sighed to himself. No longer could he even be satisfied, his boredom had reached such depths.

"Enough!" he said, his voice a command, and he watched the girl emerge from the sheets.

"But you… you didn't…"

"Enough," he said again, as if it were all he could do to summon his own voice.

"Did you not like it?" she asked.

"Like it?" he shook his head. "You realize of course that there's a *war* going on…"

"Yes, of course I do!"

"Good, because I was wondering if you were just a common whore or stupid as well…"

"Aaron? How can you *say* such a thing?"

"Easy, watch… are you just a whore or stupid as well?" his voice exaggerated and condescending as if he were speaking to livestock.

And he watched as Nelle hurried on her undergarments and blouse, tears streaming down her face.

"Why do you treat me so cruelly, Aaron?"

"I don't know, Nelle. Because you're here, I guess…"

"Well I think you are the rudest, most uncouth, most ungentlemanly *cad* that I've ever had the displeasure of meeting!"

And Aaron Burr smiled.

"I'm glad," he said.

"What? You're *glad?*" Nelle was dumfounded.

"That you can speak!" he said. "I expected a *moo*…"

"You… You have to *leave* now!" she said as she began to weep. "You have to go!"

But Aaron Burr leaned back in Nelle's bed and gave her the most disarming of smiles.

"Oh Nelle, I'm sorry," he said. "I… I didn't *mean* any of those things. You know that, right? You know I was just kidding."

"What? You were... you were *kidding?*" She wiped the tears and then grabbed a handkerchief to blow her nose.

"Of course I was!"

"But they were so... *horrible!*"

"I know, I... Forgive me."

"You're... You're really sorry?"

"Of course I am! You're my girl, right Nelle?" he looked into her eyes. "Right?"

"Yes, but what you said was so mean."

"I know," Burr smiled, "but it's the war. You have no idea the pressure I'm under."

"Yes, I... okay. If you really *mean* it, that you're sorry..."

"I am. I truly am."

This was his game. He could only get excited anymore by first horribly abusing poor Nelle, and then watching gleefully as she'd eventually forgive him.

"In fact, I'll even tell you a little secret," he said, his voice suddenly soft and conciliatory.

"A secret?"

"A military secret... but you can't tell a soul. Do you promise?"

"Yes! I promise!" she said eagerly.

"Do you swear?"

"I swear!"

"Good. Come closer," he said. "Come back to bed and I'll tell you..."

"Okay."

She plopped down next to him and he realized again how much he was truly repulsed by her.

"A horrible thing happened at the camp last month," he began. "Eight men were brutally murdered."

"That's terrible!"

"Yes, but not by the British..."

"By who?"

"By whom..." he said. "The correct usage is 'by whom'..."

"Oh, I'm sorry. By whom then?"

"Actually it's not by whom but by what…"

"By what? I don't understand…"

"Have you ever heard of such a thing as a werewolf?" he asked.

"Yes! A beast from the Underworld," she said, with a mixture of excitement and uneasiness.

"A beast from the Underworld," he smiled. "A horrible blood-thirsty beast that would rip out your throat as soon as look at you!"

And he watched her recoil in fright, and then he looked directly into her large brown eyes.

"Your eyes," he said, "they're such nice shade of brown."

"Really?"

"Like my hand after I wipe my arse!" he broke out laughing.

"Aaron…"

"Come 'ere, my finely shaped slattern. Do you know what a slattern is, my darling?"

"No…"

"Ha! I didn't think so. Strumpet? Trollop? No?" He saw that she was still uncomprehending. "Slop-jar? Jizz-bucket?"

"That's not very nice, Aaron! You said you weren't going to be mean anymore!"

"Mean? I'm not mean, Nelle, I… I *love* you, don't you see? And love makes us say things that we normally wouldn't say."

"You *love* me?"

"I do, Nelle. I truly do… So let me see those titties of yours again!" he said. And he reached over and tore open her blouse. "Yes sir, the best tits in the Continental Army! And the best quim as well! Come, Nelle," he smiled to himself, "I think it's time me and them got reacquainted…"

11 April 1778
10 am
Valley Forge

The mere thought of Nelle Watson gave him a splitting headache, and Colonel Aaron Burr was in an even worse mood than usual when some barefoot private accosted him.

"Colonel Burr?"

"What is it, Private? And this better be good, because you look suspiciously like a deserter to me."

"Me? No sir, I'm no deserter, sir!"

"Then what is it?"

"Forgive me, sir, but I heard from the men that you were interested in information."

"Information?"

"Regarding 'The Massacre', sir."

Burr's eyes lit up.

"What is your name, Private?"

"Private Solomon Bundy, sir!"

"So, Solomon Bundy, do you *know* something?"

"I... overheard something, sir. Something that I shouldn't have... overheard I mean."

"Out with it…"

"But…"

"What is it now, Private? You are taxing my patience…"

"I was wondering, sir, in exchange for, you know, the information if you would be so kind as to… you know, get me a nice pair o' boots, sir? As you can see I don't have any to speak of…"

Burr shot a cursory glance at the man's feet.

"Pretiosum quod utile…"

"Sir?"

Aaron Burr let out an exhausted sigh.

"What is useful is valuable…"

"Yes sir."

"So out with it! I don't have all day!"

"Yes sir! A week or two ago, I can't remember which, I went up to General Washington's tent to, you know, ask him about the boots, to see if…"

"More with the boots!" Burr drew his pistol from its holster. "If I hear one more word about your boots, Private…"

"Yes sir…"

"So…"

"I'm… I'm very nervous, sir. I… I forgot what I was going to…"

"Oh for goodness sake!" And Burr pointed his pistol at the Private's forehead.

"Oh, I remember now, sir! It was the General and Alexander Hamilton! I was outside the tent…"

"Washington's tent?"

"Yes sir."

"And Hamilton was there?"

"Yes sir!"

"And I suppose you couldn't help but overhear…"

"No sir. I mean, yes sir. I mean…"

"Spit it out, Private! What did they say?"

"Washington's new house…"

"The Musgrave Farm? Everyone knows that." And Burr cocked the hammer of his pistol.

"Yes sir, but Hamilton is going there *tonight!*"

"Tonight?"

"An hour before the full moon, sir. Before it rises."

"What is he doing that for?"

"To lock the basement door."

"What?"

"And in the morning he's supposed to come back and *unlock* it. Hamilton, that is."

"What are you talking about? This makes no…"

"There's something strange in the basement, Colonel, sir…"

And this caught Burr's attention.

"Strange? How so?"

"The General, he had this big iron cage brought down there, to the basement."

"Iron cage?" Burr took a step back. "Are you sure about this, Private?"

"Yes sir! Absolutely sir!"

"And you say Hamilton is going there *tonight,* an hour before the full moon?"

"To lock the basement door, sir."

There was a long pause as Aaron Burr's mind raced. And then almost as an afterthought he noticed that Private Bundy was still there.

"Well, Bundy, it looks like you got your wish." Burr glanced around and hailed the first officer he saw. "Captain…"

"Captain Ferguson, sir."

"Captain Ferguson, I'd like you to take this man here and find him a nice new pair of boots."

"Colonel?"

"Is my order unclear, Captain?'

"Um, no sir!"

"Good. Because if I see this man later on without new boots I will make *him* a Captain and *you* a Private! Is that clear?"

"Yes sir!"

The Captain stood there as if in limbo.

"Well, go on then! Run along!"

"Yes sir!"

"And you too, Private."

"Thank you, sir!" said Private Bundy, already imagining a pair of brand new boots cradling his sore, callused feet.

11 April 1778
7 pm
The Musgrave Farm
The first night of the full moon

The weeks before the full moon were the hardest that George Washington had ever experienced. His head constantly felt as if it would split apart. He was nauseated and dizzy. His every muscle and limb ached unbearably, and his stomach felt as if a burning hot cinder had been placed inside. And at night during the little sleep he was able to get he had explicit nightmares of blood and murder. And now he could barely contain himself as he waited for Alexander Hamilton to arrive at the Musgrave farmhouse. An hour before the full moon's rise, his order had been given, which meant seven o'clock. But the General found himself obsessively checking his pocket watch every few minutes from six-thirty on. There was a profound sense of the unreal in that cold, windowless stone basement. After all, here he was, standing in the dark inside an iron cage, waiting to… to change. He still found it nearly impossible to believe, especially since his wounds had practically healed by now, not even leaving any scars. But he had seen it with his own eyes; he had felt its teeth pierce his flesh. Washington shuddered, and then he heard himself laugh as he imagined what the Continental Congress would think. Surely if they saw him as a werewolf they would give him anything he wanted!

And then he heard the door upstairs, the footsteps across the wooden floor, the sound of the padlock locked tight. But he waited until he heard Hamilton leave before he removed his clothing. Then he locked the cage door and placed the key in his waistcoat pocket, and then he folded his clothes gently and placed them on the floor in the far corner. And now all that was left was to wait for the full moon. Another hour. He wanted to make sure that Hamilton was well away by the time it happened.

At 8pm the clock upstairs began to chime, loud peeling bells like in a church. But before the clock struck four George Washington felt the change coming on. At first his body was covered with sweat, then what felt like needles piercing his skin all the way to his face and into his eyes. Then he started tearing at his own flesh, as if to rip out the pain that was growing more intense with every second. A sharp cracking sound as he felt his spine moving, shifting its position within his back. His arms and legs began to distort as well, the muscles, the bones expanding, mutating into new and terrible shapes. And his eyes became inflamed, burning into his head, so hot as if they would come out the other side. And at this, Washington's mind was no longer his own but had become that of a beast. He was unaware of the fur that sprang out and covered his skin, of the hump on his back, of his teeth becoming fangs, of his fingernails becoming claws. All this happened in the mind of the werewolf, and when the transformation was complete all it wanted was to be free. The monster clutched at the bars, it tried to rip them out, but the cage was strong. And unable to escape, the beast looked upwards towards the sky, where the moon was beyond this ceiling, these walls, and it opened its mouth and howled like a wolf, but with the indescribable pain and unutterable sadness of a man trapped inside.

11 April 1778
9 pm
The Musgrave Farm
The first night of the full moon

The house was dark when Aaron Burr arrived. And after a brief search he found the door to the basement. Another padlock. No matter. His pistol was drawn and fired, the lock blasted apart. Opening the door he saw the darkness that lie in wait, so he lit a lantern and held this in his hand as he walked downstairs.

The room had a musty smell, of mildew and damp, but something else—a kind of musky, cloying, animal scent. When he came to the foot of the stairs he took another step onto a dirt floor. It was soft, and for a moment he smelled the earth as well, but then that strong animal smell again as he took another step and saw the cage. At first it seemed empty, but then he heard a low growl getting louder. And as he took another step he heard a terrible scream and into the light appeared a beast so foul, so repugnant, so startling that Aaron Burr stepped backwards, lost his footing, and tumbled to the floor. And from the ground he heard the rattling of the bars, as if any minute the monster would break through. Burr's hand shook uncontrollably as he reached for the lantern, all the while the screams and growls grew more desperate. But a moment later the lantern was relit and Burr looked back at the cage. The beast's eyes glowed red in the dim light, and when they caught his gaze he felt that his heart might indeed burst from his ribcage. But after a few more minutes the beast seemed to calm down, and it retreated once again into the shadows. And then Aaron Burr's mind began to piece it together.

Von Steuben had a cage just like this at *his* hut. And then came 'The Massacre'. They thought it was a wolf.

"They were almost right," he said out loud. "So the Baron killed those men… which means that he also attacked someone else, someone who he bit but who didn't die…"

He stood up now and took a step closer to the cage.

"Someone who becomes a monster when the moon is full…"

Holding the lantern, he walked around the cage until the light caught the shadowy image of a uniform in the corner—the uniform of a General in the Continental Army. And at that, the beast rushed the cage again and crashed into the bars, but this time Colonel Burr stood his ground.

"So, General Washington I presume… Forgive me for arriving unannounced… And if you don't mind me saying so, sir, you smell."

He took another step closer.

"So this is the big secret! And I can see why."

Burr scrutinized the beast, trying to discern the slightest bit of George Washington inside, a scintilla of his humanity, but there was nothing. Just a mindless beast before him, a complete and utter savage. He thought it thrilling that such a thing could exist!

"God indeed has a trick or two up his sleeve," he said.

And he gazed at the monster that had been his General. How powerful it was! How vicious! Surely it could destroy a squad of men, perhaps an entire platoon single-handed. To have a weapon such as this in one's arsenal would make he who possessed it a rather dangerous and formidable person. A person to whom the word "no" would never be spoken. A person to whom a kingdom or an empire would not be out of reach.

"I wonder, General," he said, "does it hurt? When the change takes place?"

He searched the beast's eyes.

"Well, I suppose I'll find out..."

And he walked up to the cage, took a deep breath, and boldly stuck out his arm, and immediately the creature attacked. It stuck its claws in like a harpoon and pulled him closer through the bars. And then Aaron Burr felt its fangs dig into his flesh. For a moment he closed his eyes before wresting his arm away from the snapping bloody jaws.

He was speechless now as he stood against the back wall, his bloody arm illuminated by the lantern's glow. He took several more deep breaths, and then he looked back at the beast.

"We are members of a rare fraternity, General, you and I... *Le Pacte des loups...*"

With that, Colonel Aaron Burr left the house in darkness, the cries of the caged beast replaced with the hoof beats of his horse as he galloped back to Valley Forge.

12 April 1778
6:30 am
The Musgrave Farm

The first thing George Washington noticed after he opened his eyes was that his headache had gotten worse. The pain shot through his body like a red-hot skewer. But he was still in the cage—that was good. That meant that he hadn't harmed anyone. But then he noticed the blood on the dirt floor in front of the cage.

"What? No! No!"

He thought of Alexander Hamilton. Perhaps he had come down here for some reason and had gotten too close to the cage.

"Hamilton!" he cried out. "Hamilton!"

Washington hurriedly got dressed. Then he opened the cage door and studied the blood for a moment longer before dashing upstairs. To his surprise the door was opened, and when he looked around he saw the destroyed padlock on the floor.

"Burr!" he said, the name spit out like an imprecation.

And then he heard boot steps on the porch, the front door swinging open.

"General!" Alexander Hamilton nearly gasped.

"Colonel, I am... pleased to see you!"

"And I you, sir, but... might I ask..."

"Colonel, tonight I would like an armed guard placed outside on the porch, from one hour before moonrise until one hour after dawn. Can you handle this for me, Colonel Hamilton?"

"Yes sir!"

"And under no circumstances is he or *anyone* to come into the house. Is that clear?"

"Yes General!"

"Good."

"And the padlock, sir?" he motioned to the lock on the floor.

"Shoddy workmanship, Hamilton... they don't make 'em like they used to."

"Yes sir," Colonel Hamilton nodded.

12 April 1778
8 pm
Nelle Watson's bedroom
The second night of the full moon

"Flowers, Colonel Burr? This is indeed a surprise!"

"I wanted to make up for the other night," he explained, "for my rudeness."

Nelle smiled to herself as she led him inside. Despite his horrible moods and the fact that at times he treated her abysmally, Nelle Watson still held out hope that one day, when this war was over, she might become Mrs. Aaron Burr.

"How's this?" she asked, putting the flowers in a vase.

"Beautiful... like you, Nelle."

"Aaron, I... It's so good to see you like this. I... I'm so pleased!"

"I'm glad, because I want this night to be special. The most special night of our lives! Come here..."

Nelle obliged, and moments later they were in her room, naked in bed. And as Aaron Burr moved above her he kept stealing glances out the window at the night sky.

"Any minute now!" he said.

"Oh darling, can you go just a little longer?" she asked, as she looked up at his face. "You are so handsome! I do enjoy looking at your face!"

"I'm sure you do," he smiled to himself.

Another glance outside. There it was, the full moon. He had never noticed how beautiful it was, and suddenly he felt as if he could make love to a *hundred* women!

"That's it! Faster!" she said. "Oooh yes!" And she closed her eyes.

The change was exhilarating. His body infused with strength, power, lust. He had become a kind of sexual engine moving above her, faster and faster, like a piston out of control.

"Oh yes!" Nelle moaned. "YES!"

And then she opened her eyes and saw his face.

"Aaron! What's happened to your eyes?" she asked. "They're… They're *red!*"

But he was oblivious as the change had overtaken him, and Nelle watched as he mutated before her eyes. She tried to push him away but he was too strong.

"Aaron, what's *happening* to you?"

And then the terror set in. She shut her eyes tight as if it were a nightmare, but when she opened them again he had become a monster, a wolf, but still inside her, still thrusting away. And then she heard the beast moan in a kind of delirium as she felt its tremor throughout her body. She hit it with her fists, she swung her arms with all her might to try and escape its grasp but it was too powerful. And then it turned its awful head and looked down at her—its red eyes like gazing into the depths of Hell—and Nelle began to cry. The beast opened its jaws now. She felt its hot, foul breath on her skin.

After it was through the monster saw the full moon outside and it crashed through the window glass and disappeared. And what was left of Nelle Watson was scattered in pieces over the bed and the floor. But curiously, her face was unharmed, her lifeless brown eyes looking out at the clock on the dresser. 8:30. A single chime rang out but went unheard.

13 April 1778
8 am
Valley Forge

Morning came and Aaron Burr felt on top of the world. He seemed to move across the camp with the strides of a Colossus. He remembered the flowers being put in a vase but nothing else and for a moment he was sad. He wanted to remember *everything*.

Valley Forge had never seemed so enchanting, and he imagined himself on a pleasant stroll through the park as he passed by some enlisted men and overheard their conversation.

"Her sister found her body."

"When?"

"Today! This morning... what was left of it."

"And this was in town?"

"Yeah. Her sister came to get her. They delivered milk to the camp."

"No kidding? What did she look like?"

"Before or after..."

"Oh, you're awful."

"Don't blame me. That's what Culpepper said."

"Culpepper?"

"And he heard it from Grimsby who heard it from one of the milkmaids who heard it from the sister herself!"

"*Jesu Christi!*" The Private made the sign of the cross.

"*Jesu Christi?*"

"It's Latin," the Private said.

And then they saw Colonel Burr and they gave him a salute.

"Colonel..." they both said.

"Privates..."

And Burr paused for a moment and smiled. But then his mood was instantly ruined when he saw Alexander Hamilton rushing towards him with a determined look on his face.

"Colonel Burr... General Washington would like to see you immediately!"

Burr let out a breath.

"Very well," he said.

And moments later he was in the General's quarters.

"Colonel Burr, how do you explain this?" Washington tossed the broken padlock from the Musgrave Farm onto his desk before him.

Burr was silent.

"Colonel, I think we're beyond games of hide and seek now, don't you?"

"General?"

"You were at the farmhouse the other night, weren't you? The Musgrave Farm..."

"Yes General."

Washington sat back in his chair.

"What did you see?"

"This, General..." And Aaron Burr rolled up his sleeve and showed George Washington his wounds, the bite marks on his arm.

"Oh..." Washington sighed deeply to himself and then turned away.

"We are brothers now, General... You and I... and Baron Von Steuben as well."

Washington was at a loss. He took another deep breath and then looked back at Colonel Burr.

"Colonel..." he said.

"Yes General?"

A long pause as Washington looked into the young man's eyes.

"That will be all, Colonel Burr."

"Yes General."

After Burr left the tent Washington took out a piece of paper and put it on his desk. He had to write a letter to his wife and tell her what had happened, tell her everything.

An hour later he was still staring at the piece of paper. "Dear Martha" was all he had written.

1 May 1778
8 am
Valley Forge

Since February, five hundred more soldiers had died of disease and malnutrition, and what little supplies that arrived had proven to be grossly inadequate. Washington had lost count of the letters he'd sent to Congress pleading for food and clothing, but today all that was going to change. Three wagons had arrived loaded with crates, compliments of the Continental Congress, and the General himself was the first on the scene to greet them.

It was a lovely sight, the many crates unloaded onto the ground, and General Washington felt something that he hadn't experienced in a very long time—joy. The first crate was pried open and what they found were winter coats. Washington smiled at the irony, as it was now the first of May, so warm as to be almost balmy. The second crate was opened. Winter coats as well, and on and on until three wagonloads of crates were opened, all containing winter coats. No food, no weapons, no ammunition. Nothing but winter coats!

"GOD IN HEAVEN!" Washington shouted.

He drew his saber from its scabbard and held it out as if to slash at Fate itself, or perhaps to cut all ten thousand winter coats to shreds, all of which had arrived six months too late. This was the last straw, and that evening he called a meeting of a very select and exclusive group of men: Baron Friedrich Von Steuben, Aaron Burr, and himself.

"I've called you here because I am sick of this war," Washington began. "I'm fed up with Congress with their thumbs up their arses while *we're* the ones who are doing the fighting and the dying! If I asked them for December they'd give me July!" he shook his head.

"General," Von Steuben said, "what can we do for you?"

"Yes General..." said Aaron Burr.

"I think you know why I've called you both here this evening. We three possess something that, while terrible and abhorrent, may in fact be used for some good. After all, what sense does *any* of it make? What sense is there that we receive 10,000 winter coats in May? I... I think we must decide what we three can do, possessing our special... gift if you will... What we can do to help bring this godforsaken war to a decisive conclusion."

"General?"

"Baron, you told me a story once of Frederick the Great..."

"I did indeed."

"How do you think the three of us would fare against a company of British soldiers?"

"If we took them by surprise, as you did at Trenton... Attack them in the middle of the night when most of them are asleep or drunk and there will be great disarray. And panic, of course, once they realize what's happening. I believe under those circumstances not a man of theirs would be left alive."

Washington paused to take it in.

"And the gunshot wounds we will inevitably sustain..." Washington resumed. "Colonel Burr and I are not knowledgeable as you are regarding what we can and cannot endure."

"While painful, the wounds will not be life-threatening. Our healing properties are greatly accelerated, General. As I have already stated, the only way to kill us is through decapitation. But these are soldiers... British Regulars trained to load and shoot their muskets and pistols..."

"Your thoughts, Colonel Burr..."

"Thank you, General. I am in accord with Baron Von Steuben. I think we should act on this bit of good fortune."

"An interesting way to put it, Colonel."

"What I mean, General, is that since this… this unimaginable thing has indeed happened, that we should look to how it may be utilized for good. After all, *armat spinat rosas…*"

"The thorn arms the rose…"

"Yes, General. And if we truly believe in the beauty of our cause, of the sanctity of liberty, of our freedom from British oppression, then we must use these thorns to bring about the end of this war!"

"Yes, Colonel," Washington nodded, "I'm afraid those are my thoughts as well."

"So General," said Von Steuben, "what do you propose?"

"The British will be coming out of winter quarters soon… if they can tear themselves away from their parties and gambling tables… We should strike at the next full moon."

"That's in two weeks, General."

"Yes. So time is of the essence. I want you both to work out a plan of attack and bring it to me as soon as possible," the General looked them both in the eye. "We'll see if we can't take what Fate has heaped upon us and use it to our favor. Let's hope that tonight is the beginning of the end for the British."

"Hear, hear!" said Burr and Von Steuben. "Hear, hear!"

5 May 1778
9 am
Valley Forge

"So what do you have for me?" Washington addressed Von Steuben and Aaron Burr.

"General, if I may be so bold," began the Baron, "the plan is this... Beginning in June the British will be abandoning Philadelphia and moving on to New York."

"How do you know this?"

"My spies in Philadelphia," said Burr.

"Your spies?"

"Well, one spy in particular. She is General Howe's mistress and... my cousin," Burr smiled.

"Ha!" Washington laughed, unable to contain himself.

"She knows for a fact that they will be leaving on the first of June, but for the rest of May they will continue to have one party after the next. A kind of grand farewell to Philadelphia. In fact, General Howe has told her of a gala affair scheduled for the night of the fourteenth of May, celebrating the arrival of General Clinton..."

"The night of the full moon..."

"Precisely."

"So our plan, General, is this," said Von Steuben. "The three of us will ride to Philadelphia dressed as British officers. And then we will go to the party. It's as simple as that!"

"The entire general staff will be in attendance," said Aaron Burr, "as well as most of the high-ranking and mid-grade officers… all our chickies and duckies in one-fell swoop as they say."

"And when the moon rises they will be decimated!" said Von Steuben. "And with barely any officers left to lead them, the soldiers will be disorganized and discouraged. And we can attack them with the Continental Army come June while they are on the move and bring this war to an end."

General George Washington sat back in his chair as he mulled it over, and then he moved forward and smiled.

"Gentlemen, my compliments on a most excellent plan! A plan of simplicity and elegance, not to mention unspeakable violence of which I am now reconciled. I am filled with hope for the first time in a long time, and I owe it to both of you."

"Thank you, General," said Burr and Von Steuben.

"Now I realize that it's only…" he looked at his watch, "shortly after nine in the morning, but if you gentlemen would do me the honor…" He brought out a bottle and three glasses. "The finest brandy I've ever tasted. From before the war. I've been saving it for a special occasion."

And a moment later their glasses were filled.

"To the end of the war, gentlemen!" Washington said.

"To the end of the war!"

And outside the tent, holding a shovel as if there were some purpose to this action, Private Solomon Bundy stood with his ears burning because of what he had just heard.

13 May 1778
4 pm
Valley Forge
The day before the attack

"Private… Private Bundy, is it?"

"Yes sir, Colonel Burr, sir!"

"I see that you received a nice pair of boots…"

"Yes sir. Thank you very much, sir! I hope my information was helpful."

"It was indeed. In fact, I have a question for you regarding a rumor I've recently heard…"

"Sir?"

"Not here. Come with me, out of the ebb and flow of the camp. After all, you never know *who's* listening."

"Yes sir."

A few minutes later they were behind one of the storage sheds, which now held 10,000 winter coats.

"Colonel, sir?" Private Bundy said.

"Yes, Private… I was wondering if you knew anything about this rumor I've heard regarding the British leaving Philadelphia…"

"Leaving, sir?"

"Yes, by early June I think…"

"Well, yes, as a matter of fact, I *have* heard that rumor, sir."

"Hmm… and what have you heard regarding my plan to infiltrate the big party the British officers are having tomorrow night in honor of General Clinton?"

"Sir?"

Burr looked at Bundy's face, grown suddenly pale as sweat beaded on his brow.

"We share a mutual acquaintance, Private Bundy… Your contact in Philadelphia, a certain Loyalist by the name of Colton Mallory, to whom you've been selling information…"

"Sir, I…"

"Please, Private…" Burr smiled, and at this Bundy began to squirm. "It is indeed a small world, Private Bundy, as this very man happens to be one of my faithful spies, and has been for quite some time! He keeps me informed of anything I need to know. Like this little bit of treachery of yours. Shame on you, Private…" Burr shook his head.

Bundy stood motionless, unable to speak.

"I should hang you," said Burr. "That would be the proper thing to do. However then the inevitable questions will be raised and… Well, I'm afraid I must take a different tack. Are you a religious man, Private Bundy?"

"Yes sir, I am, sir."

"Then I suggest you pray immediately for your sins…"

And in one smooth motion, Colonel Aaron Burr took out his pistol and fired a single shot into Private Bundy's forehead, and he watched as the hapless traitor stood still for a moment longer before toppling to the ground.

"Hmm, what a nice day!" Burr said to himself, as he noticed the spring flowers. A kind of bright yellow that reminded him of better days, of before the war, of days that would be here again very soon.

14 May 1778
8 pm
The Harcourt Mansion
Philadelphia

Red was the predominant colour this evening, with the hundreds of British officers all wearing their best crimson uniforms (and even more so once the full moon were to rise). George Washington disguised as a Lieutenant Colonel was taken aback at the extravagance, the excess. Table upon table of the finest foods: whole turkeys and hams, suckling pig, duck, pheasant, roast beef, chicken, sausage, fish. There were all manner of breads and rolls and every imaginable dessert including pie, cake, sweetmeats and ice cream. And as if this weren't enough, there was also wine and champagne from France, beer by the keg, and whiskey from the Kentucky frontier. No wonder General Howe had gotten fat, Washington thought to himself. He had a hard time keeping *himself* from the groaning board after the winter they'd just been through at Valley Forge.

"Can you believe this?" exclaimed Colonel Aaron Burr, disguised as a Captain. "The British must be doing *something* right if they can have all this in a time of war!"

"Not since the court of Frederick the Great have I seen such conspicuous consumption," said Baron Von Steuben, who was disguised as a Major.

"Gentlemen," General Washington said, "let us remember why we're here..."

At that moment a fat British Colonel came up to George Washington with a drink in hand.

"Marvelous party, eh?"

"Yes, it is."

"Lieutenant Colonel Alistair Farnsworth... Colonel..."

"Ramsey... Robert Ramsey," Washington said.

"Ramsey, you look familiar to me, old boy. Have we met before?"

"I'm sure we have. They have these things all the time," he motioned to the party.

"Quite right, old boy!" Farnsworth laughed. "Quite right! Have you tried the pheasant? It's particularly *loathsome* tonight! And the duck... practically inedible!"

"Hmm," Washington replied.

"But the whiskey! My God, I'll miss American whiskey when I'm back in England. And just between you and me old boy, I've already shipped ten cases of it back to London, so I won't run out for a while," he gave Washington a conspiratorial smile. "I'm going to miss all this when the war is finally over."

Washington nodded as Farnsworth waddled back to the buffet, and he turned to Von Steuben and Burr.

"We have to get ready," he said. "It's almost time."

"Ander... hic! Anderson!" called out a British Captain, his sights on Aaron Burr.

"I'm sorry Captain, my name is Butler."

"Nonsense! You're Thomas hic... Thomas... hic. I have these blasted hiccups!"

"Sorry, the name's..."

"Captain Butler..." Washington intervened. "You were telling me about your lovely fiancée..."

"Yes, Colonel..."

Deftly George Washington shepherded him away. And moments later the three men had made it to the foot of the grand staircase when a Great Dane intervened and began to growl, its fur standing on end.

"Easy boy!" said Washington.

But the dog showed its fangs. The General glanced around to see if they were attracting unwanted attention when Aaron Burr inexplicably knelt down before the beast. He made nonsensical sounds in a soothing way as he tilted his head from side to the side, and for a moment the Great Dane mimicked every movement of Burr's head. And then as if thoroughly nonplused, it trotted off in frustration.

"Well done!" said Washington.

And a moment later they were upstairs, in an empty bedroom where they could wait for the full moon.

"Well, gentlemen," George Washington began, "let us prepare ourselves, and remember that we do this for our country, for America."

They then removed their clothing, and just as they were stark naked there was a knock at the door. Washington took a breath, but Aaron Burr rushed to the door and opened it, his hand over his mid-section like a fig leaf.

"What is it, old boy?" Burr said. "Can't you see I'm busy?"

"Ah, quite right!" said the Major at the door, a young lady at his side. "I'll find my own room!" he smiled. "Carry on!"

When the door was closed Washington let out a sigh of relief.

"Well done again, Burr!" the General said. "Quick thinking!"

"Thank you sir."

"When this is all over…"

But then they felt the change begin as the moon rose opalescent in the window. And at that exact moment, the door that Burr had closed (which had a loose lock) became ajar, just as one of the servants came down the hallway with a bottle of whiskey for General Graydon.

"General Graydon?" She opened the door a bit more and called inside, "General Graydon, is that you?"

But what she heard was a kind of deep animal moaning.

"Well, I'll just leave it outside then..." and she smiled to herself as she closed the door.

Meanwhile downstairs the party went on, the guests all well-fed and drunk, the string orchestra playing one of Handel's more cheerful numbers. While upstairs a door exploded into splinters as a werewolf, followed by two others, burst through it and into the hallway. Moments later there was pandemonium as the horrible beasts ran through the house killing everyone in sight. Screams of terror! Blood everywhere! Chaos as men and women fled in every direction, the banquet tables overturned as the beasts crashed about in their bloodlust.

For ten minutes it went on like this until everyone was mercilessly slaughtered. And then the werewolves crashed through the picture windows and into the streets of Philadelphia.

The next morning George Washington found himself naked between two garbage bins in a rat-infested alley near the docks, and he had never felt so marvelous. Von Steuben was right, he thought. He felt as if he could win the war single-handedly! And he stood up like an athlete, like an Olympian from Ancient Greece, when he heard a voice.

"You ain't wearin' no clothes," said a dirty man dressed in rags. And at first Washington thought the man could've been a Rebel from Valley Forge.

"Yes, you are correct," Washington replied.

"Here, take my coat..." the man said.

"Why thank you, but might I trouble you for the rest as well?"

"Huh? What's that?"

And before the man knew what was happening, George Washington had picked up a hefty piece of wood from the alley and knocked him out cold. Washington enjoyed the feeling. It was exhilarating. Liberating. Never in his life had he felt so good!

Later that day the Philadelphia newspapers all ran the same story: PACK OF RABID WOLVES WREAK HAVOC ON CITY! And in a related story, OVER 100 BRITISH OFFICERS DIE IN TRAGIC FIRE! The few officers who had managed to escape ordered the Harcourt Mansion to be put to the torch, to cover up what had really happened. They knew that no one would ever believe it and they'd be considered mad as King George himself, and the only way they'd make it back to England would be in straight jackets.

Three years later
October 1781
7:00 pm
Yorktown

"Lord Cornwallis, you are punctual to the minute," said Alexander Hamilton. "Right this way, my Lord…"

Hamilton led the British commander through the house and then opened a door that led downstairs.

"The General's quarters are in the *basement?*" said Cornwallis. "How quaint."

"Watch your step, my Lord…"

Once downstairs Cornwallis saw General George Washington standing beside a huge iron cage.

"I'm sorry, but I didn't bring my dancing bear…" Cornwallis smiled in the smug self-satisfied way of the well-heeled British aristocracy—precisely what the Colonists were fighting against.

"The cage, my Lord," said Washington, "is for you."

Since they crashed that party in Philadelphia in 1778, George Washington faced another dilemma. He knew first hand the destructive power of the curse placed upon him, and that it could be used for good, for the cause of freedom. But the risk was too great. The exhilaration and exultation he felt were false. It came from an external source that was evil and he could never reconcile this. Even if it meant victory over the British he couldn't allow it to come about through some supernatural agent. Since that night in Philadelphia, Washington had kept the evil urge in check. He had confined himself for every full moon, showing the discipline and self-denial of a Spartan of antiquity, and he ordered Burr and Von Steuben to do the same. And the war from then on was fought on the battlefield, as it had always been. And thanks to Von Steuben's training the Continentals gave a good account of themselves again and again. But it was now three years later and the war was still dragging on. And General George Washington knew what had to be done.

"I beg your pardon?" said Cornwallis.

"My Lord, as a gentleman I would rather you accede to my request without having to be compelled by force."

"Am I to understand that you want me to step inside that cage? Like a beast?"

"No, my Lord, that is what *I* shall do..." And then Washington turned to Hamilton. "Colonel Hamilton, would you please escort General Lord Cornwallis inside..."

"Yes General..."

"General Washington, I must protest at this... this barbaric treatment! I was led to believe that this was to be a parley..."

"That's exactly what it is, my Lord."

"Now if you would be so kind..." Hamilton pulled his pistol and aimed it at Cornwallis.

"If you think your precious independence will come about through coercion, through force..."

"Please sir, I insist."

And moments later Lord Cornwallis was standing in the cage, and once inside he noticed bars in the middle which divided the cage in two.

"You'll notice the bars there," said Alexander Hamilton. "They may be slid out to the side if we so choose, allowing access to the other half of the cage."

"Yes, thank you for stating the obvious," said Cornwallis. "What, are you going to threaten me with a wild animal?" he laughed disparagingly. "You *are* the rustics!"

At this he noticed General Washington begin to remove his clothing and hand each piece to Alexander Hamilton. And when he was fully undressed, the General stepped into the other side of the cage, with Hamilton closing the door behind him.

"I must admit," said Cornwallis, "that I am at a loss, General Washington."

"It will all become clear momentarily," said the General. "How much time, Colonel Hamilton?"

Hamilton looked at his watch.

"Exactly one minute, General."

"In a minute's time the moon will be full, Lord Cornwallis. I am very sorry that it's come to this."

"What? What are you talking about? Hamilton! Let me out of here at once! You've both gone insane! I'll have you both shot!"

And then he noticed something strange happening to George Washington, and Cornwallis's expression reflected what was unfolding just a few feet away. At first bewilderment, then disgust, then shock, then outright and utter terror. When the transformation was complete the unholy beast rushed the bars to get at the British Lord. And Cornwallis shit his pants and began to whimper as his entire being became fright itself, as though nothing else existed.

"LET ME OUT! PLEASE! I BEG OF YOU!" he yelled, he pleaded.

"Imagine an *army* of these…" said Alexander Hamilton.

"PLEASE! LET ME OUT! PLEASE! PLEASE…"

Moments later the door to the basement swung open and Lord Cornwallis, too petrified to even be concerned about his soiled breeches, fled the house and sent his horse at full gallop all the way back to British headquarters.

The next day Lord Cornwallis eagerly surrendered his forces to General George Washington, and the war with England had come to an end.

Epilogue

Private Malcolm "Mal" Turner survived the war, leaving the Continental Army as a Corporal. Although for the rest of his days he was plagued by bad dreams relating to 'The Massacre', and his ill-fated night of guard duty.

Baron Friedrich Von Steuben, renowned for his significant role in transforming the ragtag Rebels into a formidable Army, returned to Prussia with Otto the dwarf where he retired from public life (except for the first night of each full moon).

Aaron Burr ran for President in 1800 against Thomas Jefferson, and in one of the closest elections in American history, barely lost to his rival to become the third Vice-President. Four years later he killed his nemesis Alexander Hamilton in a duel because Hamilton had threatened to disclose his dark secret. And a year after that, Burr tried to form his own monarchy with himself as King (in the territory recently acquired in the Louisiana Purchase) for which he was charged with treason—the "Burr Conspiracy" (although he was subsequently acquitted). And after the trial, disheartened and embittered, he lived a life of exile and seclusion in a remote forest on the wild frontier.

George Washington, with the war for Independence won, went on to become the first American President and one of the most beloved figures in U.S. history. For the rest of his life he kept his secret, confining himself without fail during every full moon, despite the constant headaches and torturous pain. He would later confide to his wife Martha that his self-sacrifice was the least he could do to give America the chance of becoming a great nation, unsullied by scandal, smiled upon by God, and sent courageously into the future on the indomitable spirit and goodwill of its people.

About the Author

Raised by wolves in a cave outside Rome (New York), Kevin Postupack is an internationally known novelist, existential philosopher, raconteur, and lover of women (as well as King of Spain from 1993-1997 when he was deposed by a right wing coup). When he's not writing novels he spends his days driving old sports cars and keeping clear of full moons.

In addition to GEORGE WASHINGTON WEREWOLF, Kevin Postupack is the author of the literary novels THE SERIAL KILLER'S DIET BOOK, MUDVILLE, ANGRYNASTYHOSTILE, ALL COMPACT OF FIRE, BLOOD OF THE SUN, the novella STILL LIFE WITH ABYSS, and the collection of short stories entitled THROUGH A GARDEN OF LEAVES.

O imitatores, servum pecus!

CPSIA information can be obtained at www.ICGtesting.com
Printed in the USA
LVOW041933080812

293528LV00003B/12/P